DEAD

LETTER

A HERCULEAH JONES MYSTERY

DEAD LETTER

BY BETSY BYARS

PUFFIN BOOKS

PUFFIN BOOKS

Published by the Penguin Group

Penguin Putnam Inc., 375 Hudson Street, New York, New York 10014, U.S.A.

Penguin Books Ltd, 27 Wrights Lane, London W8 5TZ, England

Penguin Books Australia Ltd, Ringwood, Victoria, Australia

Penguin Books Canada Ltd, 10 Alcorn Avenue, Toronto, Ontario, Canada M4V 3B2

Penguin Books (N.Z.) Ltd, 182-190 Wairau Road, Auckland 10, New Zealand

Penguin Books Ltd, Registered Offices: Harmondsworth, Middlesex, England

First published in the United States of America by Viking,
a division of Penguin Books USA Inc., 1996
Published in Puffin Books, 1998

7 9 10 8 6

THE LIBRARY OF CONGRESS HAS CATALOGED THE VIKING EDITION AS FOLLOWS:
Byars, Betsy Cromer.
Dead letter / by Betsy Byars.   p.   cm. — (Herculeah Jones mystery)
Summary: Herculeah Jones and her best friend Meat set out to crack the case of
the mysterious note which she finds in the lining of a second-hand coat.
ISBN 0-670-86860-4
[1. Mystery and detective stories.] I. Title. II. Series: Byars, Betsy Cromer.
Herculeah Jones mystery.
PZ7.B9836De 1996 [Fic]—dc20 96-10295 CIP AC

Puffin Books ISBN 0-14-038138-4

Printed in the United States of America

Contents

CONTENTS

DEAD
LETTER

BY INVISIBLE ROPE

It began on a day too beautiful for murder. The sky was blue. The wind from the west smelled of spring. The sun overhead was the kind drawn by kindergartners.

"Meat!" Herculeah called.

She crossed the street. Her long hair blew around her face. She laughed and pulled it back into a pony-tail with one hand.

"I hope my hair is acting like this because of the wind, not because I'm in danger."

Herculeah's hair always expanded when she was in

danger, the way an animal puffs out its fur to make it look threatening.

"I wouldn't bet on it. Anyway, you're in danger most of the time," Meat said.

"Not most of the time," Herculeah said, still smiling. "How do you like it?"

"What?"

"The coat! My coat!"

She twirled around so Meat could admire it from all angles.

"I probably shouldn't say this, but I thought you were a Russian when you came around the corner," he said.

"Thanks," Herculeah said.

She felt pleased, although she suspected Meat had not intended his remark as a compliment.

Herculeah glanced up at Meat's house. "Can I come inside for a minute?" she asked. "I have to tell you about how I got this coat. It's one of the most mysterious things that has ever happened to me."

"I guess so."

Herculeah passed him on the steps up to his house— she was always quicker than he was—and stood waiting at the door. "This is a very special coat, Meat."

"I guess you could call it . . ." he paused slightly before adding politely, "special."

Meat opened the door, and Herculeah swirled past him and into the living room.

"Meat, here's what happened. I went into Hidden Treasures because my dad gave me some money, and I wanted to spend it. I tried on some earrings. I tried on a hat with a feather. I wanted to try on some gloves, but of course they were too little."

She paused, glancing down at her hands and then up at Meat. When she spoke again, her tone of voice was more serious.

"And then, Meat, I felt myself being drawn toward the back of the store. It was like an invisible rope. I was being pulled. I had to go. I couldn't help myself."

Meat waited, caught up in the drama.

"I found myself at a rack of clothes, and my hand reached out for this coat, and I don't even need a coat. I don't even want a coat. But when I touched this coat . . ." She paused to wrap her arms across it. "When I touched this coat, Meat, my hair began to frizzle. You know, like it does when I'm in danger."

"So, of course, you tried the thing on?"

"Yes."

"If you thought there was danger involved, why would you try it on? That was a warning, Herculeah. You should have left the store right then."

Meat believed in the power of Herculeah's hair. He had seen it work.

"And it fit," she said, interrupting. "It's as if the coat were made for me. Look."

She walked around the room.

"It does make you look like a Russian," Meat said, repeating the uncompliment. "Except they don't wear bright colors. I still don't understand why you would try on a coat that could mean danger."

"Oh, you worry too much. Anyway, how could a coat be dangerous?"

"I don't know."

Meat sighed.

"But I'm sure we're going to find out."

THE WARNING

"Anyway," Meat said, "I've got other things on my mind. I can't get excited about a coat."

Herculeah looked at him. She noticed his expression. She came over at once and sat beside him on the sofa. She turned her face toward his.

"You listened about my coat, and now it's my turn to listen. You have my complete attention," she said. "What is on your mind?"

Meat wished now that she was still admiring her coat. Her gray eyes were so clear he almost expected to see his reflection in them. And what he had on his mind was that he had gone into the kitchen to get a snack and discovered a large number of cans of something called Slim-Fast on the counter. He realized that his mother was starting him on yet another unpleasant diet. He did not want to tell that to Herculeah.

He stalled for time by saying, "Oh, I don't want to bore you."

"You wouldn't."

"Yes, I would."

"You wouldn't!"

"How do you know? You don't know what's on my mind."

Actually he was boring himself. The conversation was going downhill from an already low beginning. There was silence. Meat stared glumly at his knees. "If you must know . . ." he began slowly, hoping for inspiration.

"I must."

Herculeah crossed her legs and drew the coat tight around them. She leaned toward Meat as if to prove her interest was genuine.

Before he could speak, she looked up in surprise. "Did you hear that?"

"What?"

"That rustling noise."

"I didn't hear anything."

"It came from the lining of this coat. I was doing

this." She repeated the movement. "Hear that? There's something in the lining."

Herculeah reached down and rubbed her hands over the coat until she located the sound. "There. Hear that?"

"You know what this reminds me of?" Meat said, glad to be on a safe topic. "Something my mom told me. When my mom was a girl, she felt something she thought was a fifty-cent piece in the lining of her coat and she ripped the lining open—she needed bus fare—and it was a round weight. Apparently they sew them into linings to make the coats hang straight. The bus driver wouldn't take it."

"Well, this is no weight. It's a crumpled piece of paper—maybe a letter."

She put her hand in the pocket. "Oh, there's a hole in the lining of this pocket. That's strange. I wonder if I can reach it with my fingers if I . . ."

She slipped off the coat and laid it across her lap. "I don't want to make the hole any bigger. I'm going to take good care of this coat."

She slipped her fingers into the hole. With her other hand she guided the piece of paper toward the pocket. Her fingers scissored around it.

"I've got it. I've got it!"

She pulled out the paper and ironed it smooth with her hands.

"I don't know why you're so excited," Meat said. "It's just a piece of paper, probably a receipt."

"I don't either. I can't explain it. It's just that I feel a kinship for whoever owned this coat. There's something that calls me."

Herculeah looked at the paper. She gave a sigh of disappointment.

"What is it?"

"Oh, it's just a page from an address book. There's some scribbling on it. The writing's so little and cramped I can hardly make it out."

"It's probably a grocery list. A pound of pork chops, a pound of potatoes, a chocolate cake . . ." Meat realized he was making a wishful shopping list for his own supper.

"I need more light."

Meat was glad to be of help. He clicked on the lamp behind the sofa.

Herculeah read the words to herself and drew in a breath. Her face grew pale.

"What is it?" Meat asked.

She didn't answer. She felt a chill. She leaned her head back against the sofa and closed her eyes. She took a deep breath to calm herself.

"What is it? Don't do this to me. You know I can't stand not knowing what's wrong."

Herculeah did not answer for a moment. She

couldn't. She felt as if a hand had gripped her throat. The sensation was so real that she lifted her own hand to her neck.

"There is something wrong, isn't there?" Meat persisted. "At least tell me that much. You can still nod your head, can't you?"

Without opening her eyes, her hand still circling her throat, Herculeah gave a faint nod.

"Very wrong, medium wrong, or—" He paused and added hopefully, "just some little thing?"

Herculeah opened her eyes then and looked at him.

"It's very wrong, isn't it?" he said, seeing the dread in her gray eyes.

"Dead wrong," she said.

3

"Read it," Meat said.

"Give me a minute," Herculeah said. She took another deep breath. "I feel like somebody's holding me by the throat and I can't get air down to where I need it."

"Well, it's catching. I feel bad, too. Read it. Or at least tell me what it says."

When she didn't answer, Meat held out his hand. "Then give me the paper and let me read the note."

"It's not a note. It's like a letter, the most important letter anyone could ever write."

10

"May I see it?" Watching her, he added through his teeth, "Please."

She handed over the sheet of paper.

Meat squinted at it. "I don't see how you could make it out. I can't."

He held it under the lamp.

"I cannot make out one single word."

"I can read them all," she said.

She held out her hand. It was trembling. He put the sheet of paper in it. She began to read.

I don't want to die. I can't die. He's going to kill me. I know it. He keeps coming to the door. I've been a prisoner for days. There's no window. I don't know day from night. I shouldn't have signed. Now there's no reason not to kill me. He's back! Look inside

Herculeah said, "I can hardly stand to read it. It's as if I wrote it. Look, Meat, I'm actually trembling."

"I am, too," he admitted. He was not sure whether he was trembling because of the words or the scary way that Herculeah read them. "Let me see that again."

She handed him the paper, and he peered at the small, cramped writing as if trying to make out the words. "Even though I know what it says, I can't read it. Maybe I need glasses. I always wondered how I would look in glasses."

Herculeah did not answer.

Meat glanced at the note again. "It's not signed," he said.

"No."

"I wonder who she was."

"So do I."

"We'll probably never know."

"Yes, we will."

"How?"

"Meat, I have the feeling that this letter was written to me."

"Herculeah, that's stupid. How could that be? The thing was probably written months ago, years ago. It could have been written before you were even born."

"Yes, but when she died—if she did die—she left this note hoping that someone would find it. The fact that I am the person who found it," Herculeah went on, choosing her words carefully, "means that the note was written to whoever would find it—to me."

"I'm not sure I follow that."

"It makes perfect sense to me."

"Anyway, listen to this. Maybe it's some sort of joke—like a Chinese fortune cookie that says, 'I'm being held prisoner in a fortune cookie factory.'"

"This is no joke, or I wouldn't be so scared."

"I agree it's scary." Meat decided to go on being reasonable. "Look, the woman who wrote it is probably walking around now doing perfectly normal things—trying on dresses at Belks, shopping at Bi-Lo, getting her hair done at Head Hunters." Meat stopped, unable to think of anything else women did on a regular basis.

"If she is alive," Herculeah said, "then why didn't she get this note out of the lining of her coat? And look at this pocket. She deliberately tore the lining and pushed the note through. The coat is absolutely perfect except for that one hole."

She showed it to him. "The woman took something sharp, like a key, and she pushed the letter into the lining. . . ." Herculeah trailed off thoughtfully.

"So maybe she is dead, Herculeah. What's the point of worrying about it now? You can't bring her back to life. Anyway, your father's a police detective. Why don't you just give the note to him and forget about it?"

"It's too late to get uninvolved now. I feel a kinship with this woman."

"Just because you're the same size?"

"It's much, much more than that. When I first tried on this coat, it felt right. Have you ever felt that some piece of clothing was meant for you?"

Meat, who as a boy had worn Huskies and Chubbies, and now wore clothes from the large-sized men's department, dumbly shook his head. He shook off the unpleasant picture so he could continue.

"Anyway, maybe she's crazy, Herculeah, did you ever think of that? Crazy people are always thinking people are going to kill them. It's one of the main symptoms of craziness. You don't know anything about this woman."

"Right," Herculeah continued, "I know nothing about this woman except that she was my size and that she valued life. I value life too, Meat. You can just hear how much she wants to live."

Herculeah picked up the note to read it again. She began aloud, but Meat raised his hands as if to stop up his ears.

"Excuse me, but once is enough," he said quickly.

Herculeah nodded. "I don't want to hear it either, but I might have overlooked something." She read the note to herself. "I'm wondering about those last two words, *Look inside*. Inside what?"

Meat shook his head.

"I feel that he did kill her. Look how the last word, *inside*, goes all the way off the page, as if the man opened the door and she barely had time to stuff the letter through the lining of her coat."

"It's like a message from the dead."

"Exactly."

"I had one of those once."

Herculeah looked at him.

"My grandmother sent me a Halloween card with a dollar in it. She did that for every holiday. But she had a heart attack after she mailed it—and by the time I got the card, the funeral and everything was over."

He felt tears come to his eyes at the memory. He swallowed so that he could continue. "It was a long, long time before I could spend that dollar."

"A card from the dead," Herculeah said, sighing in sympathy. "Now this."

"And what made my card worse"—Meat gave a slight shudder—"was that it was a picture of a ghost, and you opened the ghost up and inside it said, '*Boo* from Granny Hop.' We all called her Granny Hop. Her last name was Hopkins. My mom saved the card and sometimes I would be looking through a drawer for a pencil or something and I'd see this ghost card."

Herculeah nodded but she hardly heard him. She looked out the window, as if trying to see beyond the trees to a house where a woman was held captive.

Meat continued, not realizing he had lost his audience. "And I would forget about it—I'd probably repressed it—you know, like you see on TV? Something happens too terrible for your mind to accept? Anyway, my mind would be saying, 'Oh, look at this, a cute little ghost card. What's it doing in the telephone drawer?' And I'd open it up. '*Boo* from Granny Hop.'"

He gave a slight shudder and glanced quickly at Herculeah to see if she was as moved by his story as he was. He was disappointed to see her gazing out the window.

"I don't know where the card is or I'd show it to you, but I know it's in this house somewhere, just waiting till I forget about it, open it up, and—"

Herculeah interrupted before he could get out the *boo*. "I am going to find out who wrote this."

"How?"

"I don't know, but I am going to find out."

Herculeah had that look of determination that always made Meat feel like a child in the presence of an adult.

He kept looking at her. He did not doubt that Herculeah would do as she said.

Meat said, "I hope she'll be alive." This was actually a selfish thought. He was thinking of the inconvenience, no, the danger, that could be involved in tracking down a dead woman. Herculeah seemed to thrive on trouble and danger, but Meat got all he wanted of that in the halls at school.

"So do I."

"And if she is dead?" Meat did not dare to hope that would be the end of it.

Herculeah's look got sterner. "If she's dead, I'm going to find the killer."

4
HIDDEN TREASURES

"Police Department, Zone Three. This is Sergeant DiAngelo. Can I help you?"

"Hi, Sergeant, this is Herculeah Jones, and I'd like to speak to my dad—if he's not too busy."

"Chico's out on a case. Is there anything I can do for you?"

"No." She hesitated, disappointed. "Just tell him I called."

Herculeah put down the phone. "I really wanted to talk to him." She shrugged. "Though I guess it's just as well."

"Why?"

"Because he'd make me promise not to get involved."

"Smart man," Meat said. He was standing at the window. The note from Herculeah's coat and the *boo* from his deceased grandmother had made him uncomfortable.

Adding to this discomfort was a twinge of jealousy that Herculeah could phone her father anytime she liked. He couldn't remember ever talking to his father on the phone. He didn't even know where his father was.

"Maybe I ought to call Mrs. Glenn," Herculeah said, interrupting his dreary thoughts.

"Who?"

"At Hidden Treasures. She sold me the coat. Can I use the phone again?"

Without waiting for an answer, Herculeah looked up the number in the phone book and dialed.

"Hidden Treasures," Mrs. Glenn sang into the telephone.

"Oh, hi, it's Herculeah Jones. I was just in there a little while ago and bought a coat. Do you remember?"

"I do hope there was nothing wrong with the coat? Our clothing sales are final."

"No, there was nothing wrong. I just wanted to ask

if you had any idea who brought the coat in, who it belonged to."

"I don't know, but Nellie might. It was here when I took over the shop three months ago. You want me to check with her?"

"Yes. Please. I found a note, and . . ." her voice trailed off.

"Why, I'm sure Nellie went through those pockets. She told me that sometimes what you find in the pockets is worth more than the coat or the dress."

"This was in the lining."

"Well, I guess Nellie doesn't do linings." She laughed at her own joke. "Oh, I've got to go. I've got a customer. Call me tomorrow or drop by."

"I will."

Herculeah put down the phone. She looked at Meat. He was still standing at the window.

"Mrs. Glenn's going to ask about the coat and let me know tomorrow, and my dad will probably call me tonight." She gave a mock scream. "I want something to happen right now!"

Meat was still standing by the window. He paused as if making a decision.

Herculeah looked at him sharply. "Do you know something you're not telling me?"

He didn't answer.

"Meat?"

Meat knew it was impossible to keep anything from Herculeah. He said, "It's nothing. It's just that there's a man over on Oak Street who can analyze handwriting."

Herculeah glanced at him, her eyes wide with surprise that Meat had come up with something even she had not thought of.

"Meat! What a wonderful idea!"

He gave a shrug to hide his pleasure.

"No, it's brilliant. It really is!"

This time Meat didn't bother to shrug. If Herculeah said it was brilliant, then he would just have to accept it.

Her look sharpened. "Is he any good?"

"I think so."

"How do you know? Who do you know that he analyzed? You? Did you have your own handwriting analyzed?"

"Of course not."

"Then who?"

This was why Meat had hesitated before telling Herculeah about the handwriting specialist. He knew Herculeah would draw out information that he wasn't sure he wanted to share.

She waited.

He sighed. It was impossible to keep anything from Herculeah. "Oh, you might as well know. I found a letter from my dad. He had written it to me when he left home, but my mother hadn't given it to me. She'd stuck it in a cookbook, and it was an accident that I found it at all. If I hadn't wanted brownies bad enough to make them, I never would have found it."

"Was there an envelope?"

He shook his head. "No, I think he just left it on the table. It's not very long. I can say it by heart if you want to hear it."

Herculeah nodded.

"'Dear Albie'—That's what my dad called me." Meat paused. He looked down at the floor. "'D-dear—'"

He broke off and turned away. "I'm not going to be able to do this. I thought I could, but I can't."

"You don't have to," Herculeah said. She waited, watching his back. Finally she said, "And you took the note to this man?"

"Yes. His name is Gimball or Gamball—starts with a *G* and ends with a *ball*—I remember that much. He told me a lot of things about my father that I didn't know."

He still did not face her.

"Of course, since I don't know anything about my dad, I can't say for sure that he was telling the truth."

"Your mom still won't discuss him?"

"She says only, 'Good riddance.'" He turned around, his expression composed again. "Anyway, it was comforting to sit there and hear somebody say good things about my father for a change."

"Oh? Like what?"

"Well, the first moment he looked at the letter, he saw that the sentences went up at the end and he said that the man who wrote this was a person who wanted to escape routine, that he was excitable and quick to take action, that he was restless."

Herculeah looked impressed. "He told you all that even before he read the letter?"

"Yes. Then he started out with the first letter—*D*. You know, the letter started 'Dear Albie,' and my dad didn't close the *D* at the top, and Mr. Gimball or Gamball said that meant that my father was generous and openhearted. And the way he dotted the *i* in *Albie* with a kind of straight, upward line—that meant that he was good-natured and had a good sense of humor."

He broke off, then added, "Everything he told me made me wish I was living with my dad instead of my mom."

In the silence that followed, Meat's mother appeared in the doorway. Both Herculeah and Meat glanced up, frozen in shock.

Herculeah said quickly, "Oh, Mrs. Meat. Hi. We didn't hear you."

Meat's mother was buttoning her red raincoat, a

coat for all seasons. Apparently she had not over-heard—or chose to ignore—Meat's hurtful remark.

"I'm off to the post office, Albert." She held up her package. "I finished my cookbook."

"Cookbook?" Herculeah asked.

"Mom's writing one," Meat explained. "That's why she's too busy to cook anymore. I have to have . . ." he choked back the word *Slim-Fast*, "canned things."

When the door closed, Meat sank down on a chair, weak with relief. "Do you think she heard what I said about wanting to live with my dad?"

"No," Herculeah said kindly.

"Maybe not, because my mom is not the type to let an opportunity like that pass—an opportunity to say something bad about him."

"I'm sure she didn't hear. You were all the way across the room. I barely heard you myself."

"She's got good ears, though, and her specialty is picking up things you don't want her to hear."

Herculeah walked to Meat, her face bright with ex-citement.

"Meat, I am so pleased with you. This is a really good idea."

"What?" Meat was still concerned about his moth-er's hearing ability.

"The handwriting analysis."

23

"Oh, that."

"Yes, that! Where does this man live?"

"Over on Oak Street."

"Did you have to have an appointment or did you just drop in?"

"I just dropped in. He does most of his business by mail, though. He puts ads in magazines and newspapers and people send in their handwriting and he tells them about themselves."

"Then he can tell us about the woman who wrote this—and maybe about who killed her."

She drew on her coat and buttoned it quickly.

"What are we waiting for, Meat? Hurry up and get your jacket. Let's go!"

5
SHADOW

"Pretend we're having an argument," Herculeah said abruptly. "Quick, Meat, quick!"

Meat had been walking along beside Herculeah, giving more details of his father's handwriting, when she yelled this at him.

"Why?"

"Just do it! Quick! Turn around! Face me! Argue with me!"

Meat turned and glanced at Herculeah over his shoulder. "Why?"

"Not like that. I said to face me!" She gave him a half turn.

"Why?"

"Now do one of those cheerleading movements with your arms. Like you do when you're mad."

"What cheerleading movements?"

"You know. You do them all the time."

"I do not! I have never done a cheerleading movement in my life."

"Like that." Herculeah gave a sort of karate chop. "Only you do it more like this." Herculeah gave a less lethal chop.

"I do not. My arms aren't even capable of doing something like that."

"You just did it!"

"I did not!"

"You did!"

"I did not!"

Meat breathed in and out to regain his composure. Herculeah grinned.

"Well," she said, "at least we didn't have to pretend we were having an argument."

"Well, that's true." Meat put his hands in his pockets to keep them from making any more unwanted gestures. "So why were we doing this? I would like an explanation."

"I wanted us to pretend to be arguing so you could look over my shoulder."

"Why?"

"To see if there was a black car there."

Now Meat glanced at the street. "I don't see any cars at all."

"It's too late now. I'm sure he's gone, but when we came out of your house, a black car was parked at the corner. It had those smoky windows so I couldn't see if anyone was inside, but the window by the driver's side was down about that far," she said, spreading her fingers two inches apart. "Just enough so somebody could get a good close look at us."

"Oh, Herculeah."

"I'm serious. Then when we turned down Main, I glanced back and the car was getting ready to turn, too. That's when I realized we were being followed."

"It doesn't make sense," Meat said. "Why would anybody follow us?"

"I don't know," Herculeah said. "But when I saw that car, my hair frizzled. Didn't you notice?"

Meat straightened with a sudden idea. "Maybe someone's following the coat."

"The coat?" Herculeah looked down at it.

"Well, it's distinctive enough."

"Why would anybody follow a coat?"

"Nobody would. Unless—" Meat gasped.

"What, Meat? Unless what?"

"Unless it was the murderer."

"Oh, Meat."

"He thought he'd gotten rid of the woman and the coat, see, and suddenly, there's the coat."

"Oh, Meat."

"And if it was the murderer—I'm not saying it was," Meat added quickly, "but if it was the murderer, he knows about you."

"Yes."

Meat swallowed before adding the worst part.

"And me."

6
A MATTER OF LIFE AND BREATH

The sign in front of the house read:

GREGORY GAMBALLI
HANDWRITING CONSULTANT

Herculeah had passed this house many times on her way to school, but she had never noticed the sign. It was half-hidden by grass, as if the man didn't particularly want it to be noticed.

"Gamballi," Herculeah repeated.

"So I forgot the *i* on the end," Meat said. "Big deal."

Herculeah went up to the front door. Meat followed.

Herculeah rang the bell and glanced at Meat, crossing her fingers in hope of an answer.

"It's nice to see an old-fashioned doorbell," Meat said, "the kind you could stick a pin in on Halloween." Meat sighed. He didn't want to be here. The man might remember him and ask if he had heard from his dad, and Meat would have to answer no. Just thinking about it made him feel worse. He said, "Oh, he's not home. Let's go."

"He's in there. I hear him."

"You hear the radio. A lot of people leave the radio on so that burglars will think somebody's home. In motels, people turn on the TV when they go out, rather than when they want to watch something. Ask your mom if you don't believe me."

An elderly man in a sweater frowned at them from the side window.

"See?" Herculeah said to Meat. Then she called, "Hello!" She gave him a wave.

"He doesn't look very glad to see us."

The man disappeared. There was another long delay and Meat said, "He just turned off the radio. That's an encouraging sign."

The door opened slightly. "Yes?"

"We're here about a handwriting consultation," Herculeah said, pleased at how formal she sounded.

Meat decided to avoid unpleasant questions. He said

quickly, "I was here before, remember? With a letter from my dad? You said he was outgoing and avoided routine and had a sense of humor?"

"I charge ten dollars," Mr. Gamballi said, still not opening the door wide enough for them to enter.

Herculeah swirled to face Meat. "He charges! You didn't say he charged!"

"I thought you'd know that."

Herculeah said, "I've got . . . let's see"—she felt in her jeans pocket—"six dollars. How about you?"

Meat checked. "Two."

"Any change?"

"No. That's it."

Herculeah turned back to Mr. Gamballi.

"We only have eight dollars." She held it out like an offering. "But it's a small piece of paper and I am really desperate. Or—if you'll trust me—I'll bring the other two dollars tomorrow. Meat will tell you I'm trust-worthy, won't you, Meat."

"She's trustworthy."

Mr. Gamballi hesitated.

"This really is important," Meat said.

"Actually, Mr. Gamballi, it's a matter of life or death," Herculeah said, "and I'm not using that phrase lightly."

"Oh, come in, come in."

He took the money and pointed to the dining room.

"But don't you tell anyone I did this for eight dollars or that's what everybody will want to pay."

"I won't."

"Sit, sit," he said, indicating chairs. Herculeah and Meat sat across from Mr. Gamballi at the table.

"Now let's see what you've got."

Herculeah took out the piece of paper and wordlessly slid it across to him.

He held it at arm's length. "I don't like to read the words until I've gotten my graphological impressions based on the look of the writing," he explained.

"He did that with my dad's letter," Meat remarked to Herculeah.

"Though the writing is unusually small." Mr. Gamballi brought the paper closer.

A clock in the hall ticked off the time. The seconds turned into minutes. Finally Meat broke the long silence. "Have you gotten any of those—what did you call them—graphological impressions, yet?"

"Don't rush me. You want your full eight dollars' worth, don't you?" There was a touch of scorn when he spoke of the amount.

"Yes," Herculeah said.

Meat said apologetically, "I wasn't rushing you. It's just that on my father's letter, you told me right away that he was optimistic and quickly stirred to action."

"Your father's letter was probably written in his normal handwriting style. That is not true of this letter."

Mr. Gamballi looked from Meat to Herculeah. "The words are unnaturally close together, leading me to believe the woman was under great tension when she wrote this. I think she usually had a more fluid, open style. Also, there are many breaks and jerks and tremors—here, here, here—that show a lot of trauma and anxiety."

"Yes."

"The woman herself was a well-educated, sensitive person, sympathetic and emotional—I can tell that from the slant of the writing—but she was definitely under great pressure when she wrote this."

He brought the paper even closer and began to read the words. Herculeah watched his face intently, watched the lines appear in his brow.

He looked up, peering into Herculeah's face with the same intense stare he had given the handwriting. "Where did you get this?"

"I found it in the lining of a coat I bought." She patted the lapels. "This coat."

"Shouldn't you take it to the police?"

"I have—well, my dad's a police detective and I was going to tell him about it, but he was out on a case."

"Who is your father?"

"Chico Jones."

He nodded. "I've done some work for him—those anonymous letters threatening that newscaster, what's her name?" Mr. Gamballi didn't seem to expect an answer. He turned his attention back to the paper.

Herculeah said, "I'm sure my dad will help me, but I have to know more about this person now."

He looked at her. "This person felt she was going to be killed. She may have been."

"I have to know."

"And if she is dead, young lady, we're talking about murder."

"I know."

"And a murderer."

There was silence while Mr. Gamballi and Herculeah stared at each other, he with a look of warning, she with one of defiance.

Meat felt left out. He said, "Can I ask you a question?"

Mr. Gamballi nodded.

"I wanted to know if she was, well, if she was . . ." Meat paused. He had been about to say "loony tunes," but he knew Herculeah would not appreciate that. "Sane," he finished. He did not look at Herculeah because he knew she would not appreciate the question, no matter how nicely it was put. "I mean, before we start trying to find this woman, I want to rule out the possibility that it was someone who was paranoid, someone who just thought someone was after her."

"Let me look again." Mr. Gamballi's eyes narrowed. "There's a balance between the zones."

"What are the zones? I don't believe you mentioned my dad's zones."

"The upper zone shows imagination, spirit, and intellect—that's here." He pointed at the top half of some *t*'s and *l*'s. "The middle zone here—little *a*, *e*—that's the sphere of social life. The lower zone—the bottom of *y*'s and *g*'s—is the sphere of the unconscious urges, biological needs."

Meat didn't know handwriting told about those. He was definitely going to print from now on.

"There's a good balance between these zones," Mr. Gamballi said. "This writer can handle her own thoughts and feelings. She was as sane as you or I."

"I knew it," Herculeah said.

Mr. Gamballi leaned forward. "You be careful, young lady. Something terrible may have happened, and you don't want to be a part of it."

There was silence.

Meat added sincerely, "I don't want to be part of it either."

7
SHARP AS A KNIFE

Herculeah took out her granny glasses to think. She had first tried these glasses on at Hidden Treasures months ago, and the world had immediately fogged out. She found that she could think in a way she couldn't when she was looking directly at things.

She desperately needed to think now.

It was warm in her bedroom, but Herculeah lay with the coat draped over her lap. Somehow she needed to be close to the person who had worn it.

In the corner of her bedroom, Tarot fluttered his wings and moved sideways across his perch. Tarot had been Madame Rosa's parrot, but he had come to live with Herculeah after Madame Rosa's death.

"I can't pay attention to you now, Tarot. I'm concentrating."

"Beware, beware," Tarot called. This was the only word he knew when Herculeah got him, but now he had learned to say, "Oh, Mom," in Herculeah's voice.

"Hush up," Herculeah said.

Tarot bobbed his head from side to side. "Oh, Mom."

"I am not your mom and you know it. I'm trying to think."

She hooked the slim wire curves behind her ears and peered through the thick glass. While she was waiting for her mind to start working, she idly slipped one hand down into the pocket of the coat. It was the pocket with the hole in it.

Herculeah paused.

The woman couldn't have made that hole with her fingers. This coat was really put together. She would have had to use something sharp, something . . .

Herculeah remembered a thought she had had at Meat's house. She had said, "The woman took something sharp, like a key."

She drew in her breath. A key.

She took off her glasses, flung them down on the bedspread, and flipped the coat over. She ran her hands around the lining. She turned the coat over and felt the other side.

She ran her hand around the hem. "Yes!" There was an object there, caught in the fold of the hem.

She paused. "Don't let it be a weight," she said. "Don't let it be a stupid weight."

With her excitement mounting, she worked the object up to the pocket and pushed it through the hole. She scissored her fingers around it and drew it out.

It was a key.

Herculeah made a triumphant fist around it. "A key, Tarot, a key!" She opened her hand and looked closely at the key on her palm.

"I think it's a house key. It has to be!"

She was exhilarated.

"A house key! And, Tarot, a key means an answer. And maybe, maybe this key will be to the house where she was held prisoner!"

She heard the front door open. Her mother called from the front hall, "Herculeah, I'm home."

"Oh, Mom," Tarot said.

"That was Tarot, not me. I'm up here—in bed," Herculeah called back. "There's half a pizza in the fridge."

"I already ate."

Herculeah heard her mother coming up the stairs. She slid the key quickly under her pillow.

Her mother paused in the doorway. "What's that on the bed. A new coat?"

"It's not new. I got it at Hidden Treasures."

"You need a lot of things more than you need a coat. And you've got a perfectly good jacket. What do you call that color?"

"Electric blue, the woman at Hidden Treasures said. She said there was only one coat like this in the world."

"I believe that."

"I had to have this coat, Mom. It's too long to explain. I know you're tired and want to get to bed, but I had to have it."

"I am tired. I hope to wrap this case up next week." She leaned against the doorway and gave Herculeah a puzzled look. "Aren't you even going to ask me about it?"

"Your case? No."

"Why not?"

"Because I know you won't tell me."

"Still, it's not like you not to try to pry things out of me. You're not getting sick, are you?"

"Oh, Mom. I have things in my life more interesting than your case, that's all."

"You want to talk?"

"It can wait. Good night, Mom."

"Good night."

Herculeah heard her mother go into her bedroom. She reached under her pillow and brought out the key.

Her mother would have taken the key away from her. Herculeah knew exactly what she would have said. "Give me that key this minute. Keys get you into trouble. I remember the key to Dead Oaks. I remember the key to Madame Rosa's house. No more keys for you, young lady, and that is final."

Herculeah felt her hair begin to frizzle at those memories, and she swept it back into a ponytail with one hand. With the other she gripped the key.

"This key," she said, "will be different."

From the corner of the bedroom, Tarot cried, "Beware." This time he sounded as if he meant it.

8
THE LAST NUMBER

Herculeah swirled into Hidden Treasures. The bell over the door announced her.

"Mrs. Glenn, hi, are you here? It's me, Herculeah Jones."

"I'm here," a cheerful voice called back.

"Oh, great. I ran all the way from school to see what you found out."

"I'm on the phone," Mrs. Glenn called from the back of the store.

Herculeah rushed back to the desk where Mrs. Glenn stood with the phone to her ear.

Herculeah knew she should not interrupt, but she

couldn't help it. "Just tell me if you found out any-thing about the coat. This coat?" She patted the wide lapels. "Remember, I called you yesterday and you said you'd have to ask Nellie."

Mrs. Glenn held up two fingers.

"You found out two things, or you'll be with me in two minutes?"

Into the phone Mrs. Glenn said, "I do have one gin-ger jar, but it has a hairline crack in it. . . . Yes. . . . Ac-tually, if you turned that side to the wall no one would notice."

Herculeah leaned over the desk. She couldn't wait. She said, "Just tell me if you found out anything. Nod your head, yes or no. I can't stand the suspense. Then I'll leave you alone."

Mrs. Glenn nodded.

"Were you nodding at me," Herculeah asked, point-ing to herself, "or somebody on the phone?"

Mrs. Glenn pointed at Herculeah.

"Now I'm really in suspense," Herculeah said.

Mrs. Glenn shooed her off, and Herculeah walked around the store, restlessly trying on a hat, checking herself out in the mirror, opening a book of pho-tographs, and flipping through the pages.

She opened books and closed them, held earrings to her ears and put them back. She paused in front of the mirror with another hat.

"Incidentally," she said, more to herself than to Mrs. Glenn, "this is a terrible mirror. I almost didn't buy the coat when I saw myself because I looked like I didn't have a neck. There's a warp where my neck is. But if someone was shorter—which almost everyone is—they would look like they didn't have eyebrows."

She glanced back to see if Mrs. Glenn had hung up the phone. Mrs. Glenn held up one finger.

Does that mean one minute or one hour, Herculeah wondered.

At last Mrs. Glenn hung up the phone and beckoned to Herculeah.

"Nellie remembers the coat," she said.

"She does? Great!"

"Yes. Her daughter tried it on, but the daughter said she felt colder with the coat on than she did with it off—I don't know how that could be. She said it gave her the shivers. You know how young people are these days." She then realized she was talking to one of the young people and added quickly, "No offense."

Herculeah shook her head impatiently. "So where did the coat come from?"

"It was in a box—in the bottom of a box of horse stuff."

"Horse stuff?" Herculeah asked.

"Horse stuff. You know, bridles, bits, stirrups, whips—I don't know the names of what all was in there. Nellie thought the whole box was full of horse gear, but when she got to the bottom of the box, there was the coat."

"Where did the box come from?"

"She bought it at a sale."

"What sale? Where?"

"She said she went to so many sales she couldn't be sure, but she thought it was—Oh, what was the name of that street? It was a tree."

"Maple? Oak?"

Mrs. Glenn shook her head. She bit her bottom lip and then gave up. "It'll come to me directly."

"Mrs. Glenn, this is really important." Herculeah opened her notebook and took the note from the side pocket.

"Read this, and you'll know why it's so important that I find out where this coat came from."

Mrs. Glenn took the paper. "Lawd, my eyes aren't good enough to read that."

"I know it by heart," Herculeah said. "I'll recite it. It says—"

Mrs. Glenn turned over the note. "And what's that on the back? It looks like a number."

"Let me see that," Herculeah said sharply.

"Now I can make the numbers out." Mrs. Glenn pulled the paper closer to prove her point. "Eight . . . eight . . . one, no not a one . . ."

Herculeah broke in. "Please let me see that. I didn't know there was anything on the back. I can't believe I didn't turn it over."

"The next number is a two, but it's backward. Oh, I know what happened."

"Please, let me see. Why didn't I turn it over? I guess I was so upset by what the note said that . . . Please, let me see."

Mrs. Glenn closed one eye. She stared as intently as if she were reading an eye chart.

"Yes, I'm right. Somebody wrote a number on the page behind this one, closed the book, and—voilà!—"

"Please." Herculeah reached out for the note.

"I think it's a telephone number," Mrs. Glenn said, reluctant to give up the paper. "Something—that number is blurred—eight, oh, oh, two, eight, eight—only since it's backward, the phone number would be eight, eight, two, oh, oh, eight something."

She handed the paper triumphantly back to Herculeah, and Herculeah read the numbers for herself.

She started quickly for the door.

"You never told me what the note said."

"I can't stop. I've got to make a phone call."

9

PHONE CALL

Herculeah sat at her mother's desk. She had rushed home from Hidden Treasures so fast that she still had not caught her breath.

The telephone was in front of her.

Herculeah took another deep breath. She held the note up to the light and looked again at the numbers on the back of the note.

The phone number, Herculeah had figured out, was either 882-0085 or 882-0086.

She reached out her hand for the telephone. She drew her hand back as she realized she had no idea what to say if she got an answer.

She practiced silently. "Oh, hello. I found this telephone number on the back of a note from a woman. It had been torn out of an address book. And I was trying to locate this woman, and I hoped you could help me."

She trailed off. She wished Meat were with her. Meat had a wonderful telephone voice. He could sound like a radio announcer.

Her mother appeared in the doorway. "I'm out of here," she said. "Supper's on the stove." She paused, seeing the look on Herculeah's face. She hesitated, then, almost reluctantly, asked, "Problems?"

Herculeah shook her head and smiled. "No, not really. Nothing serious."

Her mother said, "Good. I'm in a hurry. I'll be late, Herculeah. Don't wait up."

"I never do."

On an impulse, Herculeah got up and followed her mother to the front door. "Can I ask you something?"

"I'm on my way out." Her mother turned. "You'll have to be quick."

"Suppose you had a phone number, Mom," Herculeah began in a rush, "and you wanted to find out who lived at that number, how would you do it?"

"Well, I've got an old high-school buddy at the phone company. You met him, Frankie Bumgardner. I've done a couple of favors for him, he does some for me."

"I know that, but suppose you didn't want to bother him—or couldn't. What would you do? What if you had to have the information right this minute?"

"Let's see. I'd dial the number and I'd say, 'Good afternoon, a new phone directory will be issued shortly,'—see, I never lie, Herculeah, they issue phone directories all the time, so one will always be issued shortly—'and I would like to confirm your listing.'"

"And they tell you?"

"Nine out of ten times they do. If not, I'd say, 'Please give me your name and address as you wish it to appear in the directory. Last name first, please.'"

"And they tell you."

"Unless they've got something to hide."

Herculeah hesitated. She had the feeling that the people with this phone number might really have something to hide. "Thanks, Mom." Herculeah turned back to the living room and her mother's desk.

"Whose number are you after?"

"Oh, it's nothing, just a number someone wrote on the back of a note."

Her mother hesitated as if she was sifting the information through her mind. Herculeah could see the moment that her mother made the wrong decision not to ask to see the note.

"Don't you stay up too late."

"I won't."

Her mother went out the door and Herculeah picked up the phone. She dialed the first number. A mechanical voice answered, "The number you have reached is no longer in service."

"Well, so much for 882-0085. Now, I'll try it with a six."

Herculeah dialed the second number. It was answered on the third ring.

A voice said, "You have reached the Poison Control Center. How may I help you?"

"Meat, guess what?" Herculeah said as soon as the phone at Meat's house was answered.

There was a long, chilly pause that let Herculeah know it was not Meat on the other end of the line.

"This is Albert's mother." Meat's mom spoke in that disapproving way that Herculeah didn't care for. "And in my day," she went on, "it was the boys who telephoned the girls and not the other way around."

"I'm so glad things aren't still like that," Herculeah said with real gratitude, "aren't you? Is Meat there? I've got to talk to him."

"Albert is—"

In the background Herculeah heard Meat's voice say, "Is it for me? Is it Herculeah?" He had heard his mom's disapproving statement about girls calling boys, and since there was only one girl who ever called him—and he realized he was lucky to have even one—he had come immediately to the phone.

"I'll take it, Mom."

Herculeah heard a brief pause in which Meat tried to take the phone and Meat's mother wouldn't give it up. Then Meat's voice came on.

"What's happened?" he said.

"Meat," Herculeah said. "I think she was being poisoned as well."

"What? How do you know?"

"There was a phone number on the back of that note—neither of us noticed it, but the woman at Hidden Treasures did—and I called it and it was the Poison Control Center. She must have suspected something— that's why they locked her up."

Meat's mother said, "Albert, are you through with the telephone?"

"No, Mom, I'm not. I just got on."

"I need to make a call."

"I'll let you know when I'm through—Oh, here, take the phone. I'll go over there." Into the phone he said, "I'm coming over."

Herculeah put the phone down and glanced out the

window. Meat had come out on the front porch of the house and his mother had come out after him. She was pointing back to the house. He was shaking his head.

The phone rang, causing Herculeah to turn away from the drama on the front porch. "Mim Jones's office," Herculeah said.

"Herculeah, is this you? It's Mrs. Glenn at Hidden Treasures."

"Yes, Mrs. Glenn."

"Well, I finally thought of the name of the street."

"Oh?" Herculeah picked up a pencil.

Herculeah glanced out the window. Shoulders slumped, Meat was going back into his house. Meat's mother threw a triumphant look in the direction of Herculeah's house.

"It's Elm Street—you know, like in that horror movie where all the murders took place. They should have called that movie *Murder Street*, if you ask me. Ever since my grandson rented that movie I haven't been able to stand the thought of Elm Street. Just the words *Elm Street* give me the creeps."

"Me too," Herculeah admitted.

Meat sat down by the telephone. His face was grim as he picked up the receiver. "Well, I've got to call her and tell her I can't come."

"Make the call and make it fast."

Meat dialed Herculeah's number. He glanced up. "It's busy."

His mother went into the kitchen. He dialed again. Still busy.

To pass the time he picked up the pencil and began to draw circles on the telephone pad.

He dialed the number again.

Still busy.

Who was she talking to?

As he doodled, he remembered that when he was little, he had had a great big pencil. The pencil was so big he had to hold it in his fist. He would sit at the table with a fistful of pencil, making loops and circles. He would dot some of the loops and cross others.

When he had filled a whole page, he would take his imitation writing to his father.

His father would take the paper at once, no matter what he was doing. He'd say, "What have we here?"

"I dunno."

"Well, Albie, let's find out."

Meat would wait for the reaction, hoping he had written something funny enough to make his father laugh.

The laughter always came, a burst of it. "This is very, very funny. Albie, you've written a very funny story. You want to hear it?"

"Yeth."

He would climb up into his father's lap. "Once upon a time there were three little wolves and this big, bad pig was out to get them."

And he would sit there absolutely mesmerized by what he had written. He would—

"You missed your chance," Meat's mother said at his elbow.

"What? What?"

"Herculeah just came out of the house. She's going around the corner right now. Seems late to be going out, doesn't it?"

Meat got to the window in time to see a flash of bright blue coat turning the corner.

"In my day, girls didn't go sashaying out at this time of afternoon—and I bet nice ones still don't."

11
THE HIDDEN HOUSE

It was late afternoon.

The shadows were lengthening as Herculeah walked quickly to Elm Street. She had been on this street before, and she remembered it as a long, curving, graceful road with spacious houses, houses with tennis courts and gardens and stables for horses.

She stopped as she turned the corner, unprepared for the change. Ahead of her lay a street in total disarray. Bulldozers, tractors, and trucks were silent, parked on either side of the street. Their day's work of tearing down houses, trees, fences, swimming pools, and anything else that got in their way, was over.

Velvet green lawns had been stripped away. The giant Tonka toys had carved the muddy landscape into a different, flatter shape to accommodate many town houses. Two houses were already rising from the bare earth: wooden structures, only skeletons now, that would become solid when covered with stones and siding.

Elm Street was now in the process of becoming one huge, expensive housing development. This sort of thing was happening all over the city, and Herculeah hated it. She valued neighborhoods.

She walked slowly down the center of the street, looking from side to side at the destruction. She paused at a sign that advertised:

Elmwood Estates
Gracious Living
3–4 Bedroom Homes from $200,000

She shook her head in dismay and kept walking. Development was happening on both sides of the street. Another sign promised:

Elmwood Manor
A New Concept in Living
Homes from $185,000

Maybe this was progress, but it didn't look like it to Herculeah.

The street was deserted. All the workmen had gone for the day. There was no traffic, but Herculeah remembered the black car that had followed her the day before. She glanced behind her.

She walked slowly. On either side of the road trenches had been dug for sewer pipes and telephone cables. These were flanked by huge mounds of red earth. The old sidewalks were buried underneath, Herculeah thought, bulldozed to pieces.

Her heart sank with each step she took. There was nothing left of what had once been here. If the woman who had owned this coat—Herculeah wrapped her arms about herself as if she were embracing a ghost— had lived here, her past had been wiped away by the bulldozers, too.

She paused for a moment, smelling the turned earth, the scent of newly cut trees, pines as well as elms. As she turned to go, she lifted her head in sudden surprise.

Beyond the few trees that had been left standing she could see an old house. She shielded her eyes from the sunset. It was a big country house. It seemed to have withdrawn from all the confusion around it.

The house had once been yellow, but now the loose dirt had turned the lower clapboard red. There were rust streaks from the ruined gutters, and black shutters dangled from their hinges.

Herculeah squinted at the house. The windows stared blankly back. She had no reason to believe this was *the* house. But she sensed it was a house like this where the woman had been held prisoner. An ordinary house, a comfortable house from the outside, but inside . . .

Drawn by something she could not explain, she turned onto the drive. There was a sign that said DANGER—DO NOT ENTER.

Herculeah stepped around it and continued slowly toward the house. She paused at the porch. Though it was empty, Herculeah had a vision of white deck chairs, rockers that might have once been lined up on the wide porch. She could see the remains of vines that had grown up the columns in happier days.

The steps were gone. Herculeah leaped nimbly onto the porch.

Again she turned and glanced quickly over her shoulder at the drive behind her. There was no one there, but Herculeah had the strange sensation that someone was watching her.

Her hair began to rise, the way it always did when she was in danger. She pulled it back into a ponytail with one hand.

She crossed the porch to the front door.

She sighed. She wished she had brought the key. She thought how satisfying it would be to put the key into the lock, turn it, and have the door swing open. That would be proof that this was the house she was looking for.

Here she was at the door, and the key was under her pillow at home.

But as she looked closer she saw that the door was not locked. Actually it was slightly ajar. She pushed it open all the way.

"Hello!" she called into the empty entrance.

No answer.

"Hello."

The sun was beginning to set, and the sky was the color of pale lemonade. From somewhere in the elm trees came the cry of a crow.

Ever since her experience in Dead Oaks, she had associated that bird with danger. She listened as the raucous cry came again. Then there was only the rustling of the trees in the early evening breeze, a sorrowful sound, as if they mourned their fallen friends.

"If Tarot were here," she said with a slight smile, "I know what he'd say—and it wouldn't be 'Oh, Mom.'"

Pulling her coat tighter about her as if for protection, she stepped inside the house. She turned and then carefully left the door open behind her.

Just in case, she thought.

12
UP THE STAIRS

Inside, the air was cold and still. The floorboards creaked as Herculeah made her way into what had been the living room.

Glass crunched beneath her feet. Someone had broken the front windows, and through the ragged panes came the scent of new earth and trees, fresh as a beginning, rather than the end Herculeah knew it to be.

The rooms she saw were empty. Everything of value—light fixtures, bookshelves, carved moldings— had been taken away, leaving a shell of a house. There would be no clues left here.

Herculeah remembered the last two words in the

note, *Look inside.* She remembered she had hoped to get in the house while it was still full of furniture. She felt she would know the meaning of those words if she could just move slowly through the rooms. She would pass a desk or a wall panel and her hair would frizzle and—

With a shake of her head she continued, making her way from one room to another. The downstairs rooms were big: a library, the walls bare of shelves; a sitting room; a parlor. All the rooms had fireplaces, but the mantels were gone.

The setting sun gave one last bit of light to the old dining room. She could see where corner cupboards had once stood. Out the window she saw a long flow of brown lawn, a forgotten garden, and in the stand of elm trees, a long, low building—a stable, perhaps.

The kitchen had been stripped of appliances and cupboards. Loose wires hung from the walls. She looked into a pantry that still had its shelves and smelled of spices.

As she moved from one empty room to another, she realized there was not a room here where a person could be held prisoner.

She opened a door just off the pantry and peered inside. This door had once led to the cellar, but the cellar itself was missing. The house had been moved from its foundation.

She went into the hall and glanced over her shoulder again, unable to shake the impression that someone knew she was in the house. Slowly taking the steps one by one, she went to the second floor.

There were six bedrooms and four baths, all as empty as the rooms downstairs. Faded wallpaper showed flowers and plaids, and in a small back room, a parade of tattered wooden soldiers.

But all of the rooms had windows. Herculeah remembered the note had said there were none where the woman was held prisoner. The woman couldn't tell night from day.

Also, there was something about this house . . . Herculeah couldn't explain it, but she had the impression that the house had been safe and secure, a place where happy lives had been lived.

Of course she would never know about the cellar.

Herculeah saw a door at the end of the hall and opened it. A musty smell filled her nostrils.

The attic.

She felt a chill of dread, something she had not felt before, not even as she peered down into the missing cellar. She tried to shake off her fear.

Why is everybody afraid of attics? she asked herself. It's just another room.

And: If you don't go up, you'll always wonder if it was the woman's prison.

And: Look how dusty the stairs are. There's nobody up there.

And: It's going to be dark soon, and it'll be worse then.

Another chill went up her spine. Someone walking on my grave. That was just an old expression, she reminded herself. Nothing to it.

She started up the stairs.

Unbidden, the words of an old camp song came into her mind. To pick up her spirits she began to sing to herself.

They wrap you up in a big white sheet.

She moved slowly. The air was stifling, probably the same air that had been here for fifty years. It could not be healthy to breathe fifty-year-old air. Get on with it, she told herself.

Drop you down about fifty feet.

She wished Meat were with her. He could have stayed hidden in the trees and given one of his famous whistles if anyone appeared.

The worms crawl in, the worms crawl out . . .

But Meat was back at home. "Where you ought to be," she heard her mother's voice say.

"Oh, Mom," she answered.

The worms play pinochle on your snout.

This song was definitely not picking up her spirits.

Gripping the handrail, she took the stairs in twos.

Yet even before she got to the top, she knew this could not have been a prison. There was too much light. Wide windows were at either end of the empty room.

She walked toward one of the windows. The floor beneath her feet was littered with dead flies and bees, the attic's only prisoners. She glanced out the window.

Not a car, not a person was in sight.

So why, Herculeah thought uneasily, do I have the feeling someone is out there? That someone knows I'm here?

The coat, she thought. Could it be the coat? She folded her arms around the front of the coat, drawing it closer about her. Had Meat been right? Had someone recognized the coat?

What if someone saw me from a distance and thought I was . . . She couldn't finish the sentence. She didn't know. Still, she shivered beneath the heavy coat. More footsteps on my grave. She forced a smile. Heavy traffic this afternoon.

She glanced one last time out the window. This time her eyes narrowed. She thought she saw a movement through the trees.

Maybe it was only a lengthening shadow, maybe it was her imagination, but the thought made Herculeah say, "I'm getting out of here."

She stepped back and then, in the final rays of the sun, she saw it.

It wasn't her imagination.

Her hair began to frizzle.

There was a car just beyond the trees.

And it was black.

13

DEATH BY BLACK CAR

Herculeah ran down the attic steps. Her heart raced. She flew across the hall and down the main stairway.

At the bottom of the stairs, she paused. She glanced out the window to see if the car was still there.

It was.

She ran into the kitchen. She remembered a back door there. She yanked at the doorknob. It came off in her hand. She flung it across the room.

A window—a window—it would have to be a window.

The window over the kitchen sink was broken, the

glass jagged. Herculeah thrust the window up, leaped sidesaddle onto the sill, and threw her legs over.

She paused to look around the outside, checking each bush, each tree, anything large enough to conceal a man. After all, whoever was following her could have left the car. He could be anywhere.

The sun had gone down behind the trees, leaving the sky the color of pale mustard. The chilly afternoon breeze had now become a cold wind. A flock of crows flew overhead, cawing.

Herculeah glanced down at her coat—electric blue, the woman at Hidden Treasures had said. It would be easily spotted. She took off the coat, folded it so that the lining was outside, the brilliant blue concealed. She rolled it into a bundle and stuck it under her arm. In one quick motion she jumped to the ground and ran, zigzagging for the shelter of the trees.

She paused there for a moment, considering her chances. She could make her way through the trees, but sooner or later she would have to come out on Elm Street. She remembered where the car had been and felt that if she could come out of the trees behind it, she could make a dash to Main Street before the driver could get the car turned around.

Jogging through the trees, her hair blowing behind her, she could hear the traffic on Main Street. She slowed as she came to Elm. She peered around the trees. There was no car in sight.

"It's gone," she said.

She was ashamed of the fact that she suddenly felt weak with relief.

She didn't want to linger. She picked a spot where the mound of dirt was lowest, climbed over, hopped the trench, and stepped onto the roadway. She brushed off her jeans, unfolded her coat, and put it on. She was loping toward Main Street when she heard it.

A car engine.

She glanced back. The car had been hidden in the trees. Now it roared out, tires squealing, coming straight at her.

Herculeah was in the worst possible place. Perhaps the driver had been waiting for that. Beside her, the mound of dirt was too high to jump over, the trench too narrow to fit in. There was no room to get out of the car's way. She glanced back again.

The car was twenty yards away.

It was gaining speed.

Herculeah had always heard that when you thought you were going to die, your whole life passed before your eyes. What passed before Herculeah's eyes was a fast-approaching bumper—it was less than ten yards away now—and the thought that she was not going to die by a black car.

She threw herself up the bank. Her feet slipped on the loose earth. She went down on her knees. She glanced at the car.

It was five yards away now.

Using all her strength, Herculeah pushed herself up the mound of earth and threw herself over the top. The car sped past, swerving on the very spot where she had stood only seconds ago. She could smell the sickening scent of exhaust.

She took deep breaths. She was relieved, but at the same time—

She lifted her head. She heard the car back up, the squeal of brakes. The car stopped. There was a whir as the window rolled down.

Herculeah waited. Her heart began to pound in her throat.

She knew the driver of the car was just on the other side of the ditch, listening, waiting for her to reappear. If she did, he would come at her again. And this time, she might not be quick enough to get away.

She ran beside the mound of earth, toward the sound of the traffic, eyes fixed on her goal, breath held. She stayed in a crouch, keeping her head well below the top of the mounds of red earth.

And then she heard the noise, the persistent whir of the engine. The car was moving too.

It moved at her pace, always just a stone's throw

away. It was as if the driver could see through the pile of dirt and knew exactly where she was.

Herculeah kept moving. Her throat was dry. The blood pounded in her ears.

She came to what had once been a driveway. Now it was just an open space.

When she crossed that space, Herculeah knew she would be vulnerable. If the driver did know where she was, he would anticipate her movements. He could swerve into the driveway, and— "and I'd be history," she said.

She took a deep breath, another, and then with a burst of speed that surprised even herself, Herculeah ran across the open space and into the shelter of the elm trees.

Panting with exertion and fear, but shielded by the trees—he couldn't get her here—she glanced at the car. With a screeching of tires, the car roared by and disappeared in a cloud of reddish dust.

It really was gone this time.

Keeping to the edge of the trees, Herculeah ran toward Main. As she rounded the bend, she could see the lights ahead, the cars, the people moving and shopping. She hurried to be one of them.

As she walked, she bent and began to brush off her coat. "And I was going to take such good care of this coat," she said.

Herculeah came to Main Street. When she crossed she looked both ways, the way her mother had taught her to when she was a child.

Then Herculeah turned for home.

But she had the terrible feeling she would see that black car again.

"You're filthy, Herculeah! Where on earth have you been?"

"Oh hi, Mom."

"Look at yourself."

Herculeah glanced in the hall mirror. "Oh, no. I don't care about myself," she said. "Look at my coat. This is my new coat! I love this coat. It's ruined."

"I've got a brush. I'll have a go at it."

"Thanks."

"But where have you been?"

"I was checking out some construction over on . . ."

She made a quick decision to leave off the name of the street. "On the other side of Main Street. That's where I was."

"I thought you'd outgrown digging in the dirt."

"Oh, Mom."

"See, that's where Tarot got his 'Oh, Mom's' from."

Her mother left the room and returned with a brush. "Take it off," she told Herculeah. Herculeah shrugged out of the coat.

"What happened? Did you fall?" With long, sure strokes, Herculeah's mother brushed the coat. "It's coming out. See?" She paused to look at Herculeah. "So did you? Fall?"

"Mom, it was very strange. I was on my way home. The street I was on . . ." again she was careful not to give the name, "is very narrow. They've dug ditches for pipes and haven't filled them in. The dirt's in huge piles, some of it out in the street.

"So I was walking along and I heard a car behind me. I looked around. It was a black car. No lights. No big deal—it was just sunset. And then the car started coming at me—right at me. So I scrambled up the pile of dirt, slipped, and fell down on my knees—that's where those two circles of dirt came from. Then I threw myself over the top. That's where the rest of the dirt came from."

Her mother had stopped now, the brush suspended over Herculeah's coat. "Do you think the driver did it on purpose?"

"Why would he?" Herculeah asked evasively.

"You tell me."

"It was dark. It's possible he didn't see me."

"Did you get the license number?"

"Not hardly. I was on my face in the dirt when it passed."

Herculeah decided not to mention that the car had tried to stay with her and that she had to make a frantic dash for safety.

"Anyway, it's over. I'm unharmed. I'm safe. I learned my lesson."

She grinned at her mother. Her mother didn't grin back. "I wish I could believe that."

"Believe it. Oh, I've got to hurry. Dad's picking me up, remember?"

Her mother was still watching as Herculeah started up the stairs.

"Oh, Herculeah—"

"Mom, I have learned my lesson, all right?"

"Meat stopped by and left something for you. He said it was important." Mrs. Jones picked up a folded sheet of paper from the hall table and handed it to Herculeah.

Herculeah unfolded it. "It looks like a Xerox of some

sort of note." She felt a quickening of interest because it might have something to do with the coat.

"Yes, that's what Meat said. He was just back from the Copy Cat."

"I wonder if this has anything to do with . . ." She broke off with a brief glance at her mother and sat down on the stairs. She read it and the paper sagged to her lap as if it were too heavy to hold.

"Oh, Mom, you know what this is?"

"No, what?"

"Oh, Mom."

"Well, tell me."

"Meat and I were talking about a note his father wrote him—the only note his dad ever wrote. Meat came across it stuck in his mom's cookbook. I asked him what the note said, and he started to tell me— he knew it by heart—but he couldn't finish. I think he was afraid it was going to make him cry. And for some reason Meat has the stupid notion that he can't cry in front of me! I've cried in front of him lots of times."

"Boys," her mom said with a shake of her head. She smiled down at the top of Herculeah's head.

Herculeah was looking down at the sheet of paper. "I know that's what this is, because it starts out 'Dear Albie.' Meat got that far. He told me his dad called him Albie."

Herculeah looked up at her mother. "Do you want to hear it?"

"I'd like to very much—if you don't think Meat would mind."

"I don't. Here goes. 'Dear Albie, I'm sorry, Pal, that I had to leave without saying good-bye. But when a man gets his big chance, he has to take it. Mind your mom now and don't ever forget me.' And it's signed 'Sweet old Dad.'"

15

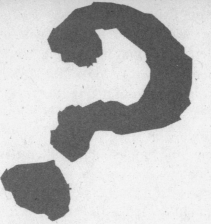

"So, Dad," Herculeah said, "I was hoping you'd wear that tie. It's my favorite."

"Actually, it's my third favorite."

"You've only got three."

"Four, if you count the Snoopy tie you gave me last Christmas."

"Which you never wear."

Herculeah and her father were in a Chinese restaurant, waiting for their food to be served. Herculeah did not want to talk about ties. Her only interest was the note that had been in the lining of her coat, but now she felt reluctant to discuss it. She was sure her father would sense she was too interested and would make her promise not to get involved.

"I'm sorry I wasn't at the precinct when you called yesterday, Herculeah. Was it anything important?"

"No, not really."

"DiAngelo said you sounded upset."

"Well, I was, a little."

"So?"

"Well, something happened that afternoon that sort of bothered me."

"Such as?"

"You aren't going to like this."

Her father looked less relaxed. He sat up straighter. "You haven't found another body, have you, Herculeah?"

Herculeah tried to ignore her father's disapproving tone. It wasn't her fault she'd discovered poor Madame Rosa murdered, or almost fallen on a body in that abandoned house, Dead Oaks.

"No."

"Well, that's a relief."

She added, "At least I hope not."

"What's that supposed to mean?"

"Just what it says."

"Go on."

"Well, you remember that money you gave me?"

"Yes, I remember the money I gave you. You called me up and said, 'Do you have any extra money?' Herculeah, nobody has extra money. There's no such thing as extra money. Even millionaires—"

"Don't give me the extra-money lecture. This is too important."

"Well, get on with it."

"I went into this store called Hidden Treasures. It's where I buy most of my stuff—my binoculars came from there and those little round glasses that help me think—but this time something drew me to the coat-rack, which surprised me because I do not need a coat. Nobody I know even wears coats. Everybody wears jackets."

"Are we at the important part yet?"

"We're getting there. Dad, I was drawn to this coat. I put it on and it fit perfectly. I took it to Meat's to show him, and he said it makes me look Russian—did you think so?"

"I'm not up on Russian fashion."

"Anyway, I noticed there was a piece of paper caught in the lining of the coat. I got it out and it was really . . . well, it scared me. That's why I called you."

"What did the note say?"

"It was written by a woman and she said somebody was going to kill her."

"Where is the note?"

The note was in Herculeah's pocket, but for some reason she was hesitant about bringing it out.

"What did the note say—exactly?"

Herculeah sighed. She felt she was making a mistake, but she pulled out the note.

"Read it for yourself," she said. She pushed the piece of paper across the table.

Her father read the note and looked up at her, his expression serious. "And you found this in the lining of the coat?"

"Yes."

"Where'd you buy the coat?"

"I told you—Hidden Treasures."

"Did the woman who sold you the coat know where it came from?"

"Not exactly—just that it was in a box of horse stuff—you know, like bridles and whips."

"Did you discuss this with your mom?"

"I couldn't. She was on a case."

Her father now gave a sigh of disgust. One of the reasons Herculeah's parents had divorced was because her father belittled her mother's career as a private investigator.

Herculeah went on quickly. "She wouldn't tell me what the case was because she doesn't want me to get interested."

"Well, that's the first smart thing your mom's done in a long time."

"Dad, the reason I called you was because I wanted to ask you to pull your files—you know, for unsolved deaths—for murders that could have been made to look like accidents."

Her father turned the note over.

"The woman, the victim, would be a woman exactly my size. You know how big I am, don't you? I weigh the same as mom and I'm as tall as you."

"I know how big you are."

"So will you please do it? Please? This is very important to me. I feel some sort of kinship with this woman."

"Yes, I'll look into it. I've already got some thoughts on it."

Herculeah leaned forward eagerly. "Like what?"

"Well, I take it from the appearance of the coat—I mean, that is not a cheap coat, Herculeah—"

"I know. I paid six whole dollars for it."

"I'm talking about the original price. What I'm getting at, Herculeah, is that the owner of that coat was not some bag lady."

"No."

"The victim, if she turns out to be one, which frankly I doubt—"

"I don't."

"The victim was fairly well-off and probably lived in a nice section of town."

"Probably a very nice section of town," Herculeah said, remembering the houses that had once lined Elm Street.

Her father glanced at her sharply, and she said quickly, "Go on. Don't pay any attention to my comments."

"I'm trying not to."

"Dad, are you going back to the precinct tonight?"

"Give me a break, Herculeah."

"Are you?"

"Maybe."

"And will you pull your files?"

"Maybe."

"And will you call me? I know the answer. 'Maybe.' Oh, great, here comes our food. Let's eat up so we can get out of here and you can get back to the precinct."

Herculeah picked up her chopsticks. "And I bet I know what my fortune cookie's going to say. 'An important question will be answered.'" She smiled.

"Or 'Keep out of matters that don't concern you,'" her father said.

And he was not smiling.

16

"I expected you to call me last night," Herculeah said to her dad.

Chico Jones had stopped by the house on his way to work. Herculeah was having breakfast.

"I got busy."

"That's good. What did you find?"

"Let me get some coffee." Herculeah watched him cross the kitchen. "Mim, you got any coffee?"

"By the stove."

Herculeah waited impatiently while her father poured himself a cup of coffee. He sat across from her, and she leaned forward over her cereal bowl.

"So what did you come up with?"

"Two names."

"Only two names? You mean there are only two un-explained deaths in this whole city?"

"Yes. Two. Be grateful. In the past twenty years—and that's as far back as I went—there have been two women who fit the picture you've given me. Two is far too many unexplained deaths for me."

"Yeah, sure, I didn't mean it that way." She put her elbows on the table. "So. Who are they? What are their names?"

Her father pulled out a piece of paper. He read from it. "Ethel Alice Stackmoore, 38, height 5'7", weight 124, was found dead of a gunshot wound, October 21, 1992, in her residence. No weapon found, no arrests."

"Where did she live?" Herculeah asked.

"In Marietta. I've got all that down here, including the addresses."

"Marietta," Herculeah said thoughtfully. She shook her head. "I don't think so. Too far away. Who's next?"

"Holly Forthright Downing, 24, height 5'7", weight 128, cause of death, brain injury caused by fall down the basement stairway at her residence. Ruling by the court was accidental death, but the case is not closed."

Herculeah put one hand to her throat. "Where was that?" she asked quickly.

He slid the sheet of paper across the table to her. Actually, it was only half a sheet of paper.

She checked the address. "Griffin?" Her shoulders sagged. "Griffin's miles away from here."

He nodded. "Is there any cream, Mim?"

Mim Jones took a carton of skim milk from the refrigerator and set it on the table.

"I can't believe this is it," Herculeah said. She kept staring at the paper in disappointment.

"What did you expect?"

"I expected better things of you."

"I hear that all the time."

"Herculeah, you're going to be late for school."

"I'm leaving right now."

Herculeah went into the hall, put on her coat, and picked up her books.

"Aren't you even going to say thanks?" Chico called after her.

She stuck her head back into the kitchen. "Yes, thanks for trying, Dad."

"You're welcome, hon."

Meat was waiting for her across the street. She ran to him. "Oh, Meat, disappointment. My dad came up with nothing, absolutely nothing—one woman in Marietta and one in Griffin—both of which are too far away. Here. See for yourself."

"Yeah, right. Well, I guess that's the end of it." Meat was not disappointed in the results—actually he was relieved.

"It is not the end of it," Herculeah said forcefully. She looked down. "Oh, I forgot my library book and it's due today. Wait for me."

Herculeah entered the house and picked up her book from the hall table.

In the kitchen, her parents were talking quietly—not arguing. Herculeah paused. She didn't want to disturb them. She loved it when her parents were like this, drinking coffee together, talking. She could almost believe they had once been in love.

"I wish you hadn't given her those names, Chico," her mother was saying.

"Why?"

"Herculeah takes too many chances—you know that. She gets too caught up in things that don't concern her."

"I wonder where she gets that from?"

"Both of us."

They laughed. In the hall, Herculeah smiled.

"You don't have to worry, Mim."

"I can't help it."

"One of the names I gave her was in Marietta, the other in Griffin."

"Well, that makes me feel a little better, though a matter of miles wouldn't stop Herculeah."

"This is the one I didn't give her." Herculeah heard her father take a sheet of paper from his pocket—the other half of the sheet of paper, probably—and hand it to her mother.

"Elm Street," her mother read.

Herculeah waited, her heart in her throat. How lucky it was that she had not told her mother the black car had been on Elm Street.

"Amanda Cole."

Herculeah took a deep breath. She clapped one hand over her mouth to keep herself from whooping with triumph. She slipped quietly out the front door and flew across the street.

"I got it, Meat! I got it!"

Meat paused. Herculeah's face was so flushed he thought she was talking about a disease.

"What?"

"The name! The name!"

"What name?"

"The murdered woman's. Her name was Amanda Cole. Aren't you excited, Meat? This means we're almost there."

"Where?"

"To the murderer, Meat, to the murderer."

17

OBITUARY

"I'm getting tired of looking at obituaries," Meat said.

"Well, I'm not," Herculeah answered.

"They're depressing."

"Not to me."

"I bet they are to the people they're about."

"The people they're about can't read them. They're dead."

"Well, I've got to take a break. Let me know when you find something."

Meat's break consisted of leaning back in his chair and closing his eyes. Still, he had to glance at Herculeah occasionally to see how it was going.

Herculeah and Meat had come right to the periodical room of the public library after school. The city newspaper was on microfilm, and Herculeah was now threading in the reel for 1991, January–June. Herculeah was peering intently at the screen.

"What month are you on now?" he asked.

"Open your eyes and see."

"I'm on a break."

"January."

"What year?"

"Ninety-one."

"How long are we going to keep this up?"

"We're going to keep it up until we find what we're looking for."

Herculeah was getting ready to roll directly to the obituary page when an article caught her eye. "Noted Resident Dies in Accident." Then she saw the subheadline and read it aloud: "Amanda Forrest Cole, Sportswoman and Philanthropist, Dead at 45."

Meat opened his eyes. "Did you say, 'Dies in accident'?"

"Yes. Accident."

"What date?"

"See for yourself."

Meat peered at the date.

"Accident, Herculeah," he said. "That means the killer got away with it. If the newspaper says—"

"Be quiet, I've got to concentrate."

Meat leaned forward and began to read aloud, "'Mrs. Amanda Forrest Cole, widow of Franklin Cole, was pronounced dead on arrival at Grady Hospital early yesterday morning, following a fall from her horse.'"

"Meat, read to yourself."

He read: "Mrs. Cole, who had been in ill health for several weeks . . ." to himself, but then he found he missed the sound of his own voice.

He broke off reading to comment, "I just have to read one more thing aloud and make one comment."

"Oh, go ahead."

"'Mrs. Cole, who had been in ill health for several weeks . . .'"

"And what's your comment?"

"My comment is that anybody would be in ill health if they were being poisoned. That's about the quickest road to ill health there is."

"I agree."

Meat nodded as if he had made an important point and went back to reading to himself.

"Mrs. Cole left the house sometime after lunch against her doctor's advice. No one on the premises at the time—a servant, a stable boy, and Mrs. Cole's nephew, Roger Cole—saw her depart. 'If we'd seen her, of course we would have stopped her,' Roger Cole said. 'She was in no condition to be on a horse.'

"Mrs. Cole was not missed until supper time, when one of the servants knocked on her bedroom door. There was no answer and the room was empty. An immediate search of the house was begun, and when it was discovered that Mrs. Cole's horse was missing, the search widened to include the neighboring horse trails. Her body was found at 7:00 P.M. and she was taken to the hospital, where she was pronounced dead.

"A formal inquest into the death will be held on Friday."

"Well, at least they're going to have an inquest." Meat leaned forward. "Is there an inquest section?"

"I hope so."

Herculeah turned through the film so quickly the ads and funny papers and TV listings and front pages all ran together in one gray blur. Suddenly Herculeah stopped and rewound the film.

"There's a picture of her," Herculeah said.

"How do you know that's her? We can't even see the caption."

"I know."

Herculeah rolled the rest of the newspaper page into view. "Mrs. Amanda Forrest Cole, shown at the Bennington horse show in 1990, died last Saturday. Her death, which has left the community saddened, was ruled an accident yesterday."

91

"He did get away with it," Meat said.

"Not yet."

She was still staring intently at Amanda Cole's face. "I think she looks like me."

Meat looked from the newspaper picture to Herculeah and back. "No, you're younger and"—he leaned closer—"she doesn't even come close to you in the hair department."

"Not in that picture. She wasn't afraid there."

Herculeah leaned back in her chair.

"That came later."

"There are a lot of suspicious things in this report about the inquest," Herculeah said as she and Meat left the library. Herculeah had the printouts of the obituary and inquest rolled up in one hand. She shook them for emphasis.

"Such as?" Meat said.

"Well, for one thing, that housekeeper."

"What about her?"

"The housekeeper said that Mrs. Cole doted on her nephew, that she 'wouldn't let anyone take up her meals but Mr. Roger.'"

"What's suspicious about that?"

"Plenty. Anyway, I would like to have questioned the housekeeper myself. I'd like to know if Mrs. Cole told her that or 'Mr. Roger' did. I mean the whole time 'Mr. Roger' was taking up her meals, Amanda Cole could have been locked away somewhere else. He could have been eating the meals himself."

"You're too suspicious."

"You're not suspicious enough. And the last time the housekeeper actually saw her was Monday. Monday! What was it the housekeeper said?"

Herculeah unrolled the sheets of paper. "The housekeeper said, 'Mrs. Cole didn't seem herself.' And she never saw her again. She left for the weekend. She offered to stay on, but 'Mr. Roger' said Mrs. Cole wouldn't hear of it. 'Mr. Roger' said she was feeling better and might go for a ride the next day. 'Mr. Roger' winked at her and said, 'But we aren't going to let her do that just yet, are we?'"

Herculeah and Meat walked half a block in silence. "You know what I think happened?" Herculeah asked.

Meat waited.

"I think she was locked up somewhere that whole time. I think she was 'Mr. Roger's' prisoner. Maybe one of the servants was in on it with him. They took her prisoner after the housekeeper saw her on Monday, held her there until the housekeeper left on Friday, and then killed her. You know what else I think?"

Meat waited.

Herculeah gasped.

"What is it?"

"I just saw something in that store window."

"What?"

"Promise you won't turn around and look."

"I promise. What is it?"

"Meat, I saw the reflection of a black car, the same kind of car that tried to run me down."

"Where?"

Meat turned around at once, stepping back closer to the buildings. "I don't see any black car."

"I told you not to look!"

"I couldn't help myself."

"I know it was the same car. Look how my hair's beginning to frizzle."

"Well, it's gone now."

"We don't see it now. That doesn't mean it's gone. It could have circled the block and be planning to run us down at the next intersection."

Herculeah and Meat walked slowly, cautiously. At each intersection they paused, looking in both directions in a way that would have made their mothers proud, half expecting to see the black car, engine revving, waiting to catch them in the crosswalk.

"Well, at least we're almost home," Meat said finally. "And we don't have any more streets to cross."

They turned the corner onto the street where they lived. They stopped abruptly.

The low, black car was parked in front of Herculeah's house.

"Is that it?" Meat asked, whispering although there was no one to overhear.

"It looks like it," Herculeah answered.

"What are you going to do?"

"I don't know."

"You have to do something. He's probably seen us. We can't just stand here."

Herculeah's head went up purposefully.

"I'm going to do what I was planning to do all along: go into my house."

"I'm not sure that's a good idea."

"It's my only idea. Are you coming?"

"Well, sure. I guess."

They walked the rest of the block quicker than they would have liked. They each showed their tension in different ways—Herculeah by slapping the papers she held against her leg, Meat by keeping up a steady stream of conversation.

"We could cross over and go to my house, Herculeah, want to? Let's do it. My mom's probably home and yours isn't. Come on, there's no traffic. Now's our chance. Only maybe we better not. He could back over us. It wouldn't be easy, but—"

Herculeah interrupted. "When we pass the car, don't look at it." She spoke through her teeth.

"I'm not," he said even as he sneaked a look out of the corner of his eye. "Anyway I wouldn't be able to see anything through the tinted glass."

Side by side, shoulders touching, Herculeah and Meat turned and started up the stairs to Herculeah's house. They heard a car door open and close behind them.

"Excuse me," a male voice called.

Herculeah turned, her gray eyes dark with suspicion. "Are you speaking to me?"

"I sure am."

The man getting out of the black car was tall and handsome, his smile Hollywood white, his eyes as blue as his cashmere sweater. These things doubled Herculeah's suspicions, tripled them.

The man came forward with easy steps. He parted his lips in another dazzling smile. He put out his hand.

Herculeah smelled an after-shave that was probably called something like "After Tennis" or "After Golf," or "After Attempted Murder in a Black Sports Car."

"Let me introduce myself," he said.

Herculeah looked at his outstretched hand warily. She made no move to take it.

"My name is Roger—Roger Cole."

19

MEGA-SLEAZE

"What a sleaze! What a terrible sleaze!" Herculeah said as she closed the door of her house.

"Be quiet. He'll hear you."

"I hope he does."

Herculeah stomped into the living room. She crossed to the window and watched the man get into his car.

"Multi-sleaze!" she called. "Mega-sleaze!"

Meat said, speaking almost to himself, "Some of what he said made sense."

Herculeah swirled to face Meat. There was such

fury, such disbelief in her expression that he wished he had not spoken at all. He took a step backward and added quickly, "But then again, maybe it didn't."

Herculeah began to imitate Roger Cole's voice. "'I think I owe you an apology, young lady.' Smile. Wink. I hate men who wink for no reason. It's so gross."

Meat had been present during the entire conversation, but he could see that Herculeah wanted to tell her version.

"'I understand from the man who was driving my car the other day that you two had an unfortunate encounter. The driver's the watchman on my Elm Street property, and we've had a lot of trouble with vandals and trespassers lately.'"

"That was the part that sounded sort of true," Meat said.

"Are you telling this or am I?"

"It's all yours."

She went on in Roger Cole's voice. "'He just wanted to scare you.' Huh, he wanted to kill me! 'He's not used to my car and didn't realize how close he came. He stayed around to apologize but you ran off.' You bet I ran off. I wouldn't be alive if I hadn't.

"Anyway, Meat, he didn't come here to 'apologize.' The only thing he really came over to say was, 'It would probably be a good idea if you stayed away from the property from now on. I wouldn't want anything to happen to you.' Wink. Smile. I HATE men who wink."

Meat had never winked at anyone in his life, but now his eye felt like it was getting ready to. Winking would be the worst thing he could possibly do. He was saved from this fate by Herculeah's mom.

"Who, besides me, doesn't want anything to happen to you?" she asked.

Herculeah glanced up in surprise. She didn't answer.

Meat did it for her. He said quickly, "The man in the black car, Mrs. Jones. Did Herculeah tell you about him trying to run her down?"

"Be quiet, Meat," Herculeah said, singing the words. "I'll tell it in my own way."

"Actually," Mrs. Jones said, "I'd like to hear Meat's version." She turned her cool gray eyes—Herculeah's eyes, he realized with a start—on him.

Meat always felt important when he gave information to Herculeah's parents: a private eye and a police lieutenant. It was as close as he would ever come (he hoped) to giving real testimony.

He glanced at Herculeah. She had turned her back on him. Mrs. Jones, however, was giving him her private-investigator look, the one that made people spill their guts.

"Meat?"

"Well," he began, "the man who tried to run Herculeah down the other day on Elm Street, he—"

Meat didn't get to finish his testimony.

"Elm Street! Elm Street!" Mrs. Jones cried, turning on Herculeah. "You didn't tell me this happened on Elm Street. You said on the other side of Main."

"Mom, this was on the other side of Main Street. It depends on which side of the street you're on."

"Don't give me any of your double-talk. You were on Elm Street and you were looking for this woman you think was murdered."

"I don't think she was murdered, I know she was."

"I am not interested in your opinions. I want one thing from you, young lady."

"I hate it when you call me young lady."

"I'm not interested in your likes and dislikes. I am interested in one thing and one thing only. You are not to set one foot on Elm Street. Is that clear?"

"Oh, Mom—"

"I want your promise."

"Mom—"

"I'll get your father in on this if I have to. If I can't stop you, the police can."

"Oh, all right," Herculeah said quickly. "Don't join forces with Dad. I will not set one foot on Elm Street again."

"That's a promise?"

"Yes."

She pointed at Meat. "I want you to promise me the same thing."

"I promise." Meat spoke so quickly it sounded like one word.

"Now, about this man in the black car, he came to this house?"

Herculeah's back was still turned.

"Meat?"

"Well, Mrs. Jones, the man who tried to run her down was the watchman—this man just wanted to apologize. He said the watchman didn't mean to. He thought she was a vandal and wanted to scare her. But we don't believe that."

"Oh?" Mrs. Jones gave him another of those spill-your-guts-or-else looks. He spilled.

"Because after Herculeah fell over onto the other side of the dirt, the black car stayed with her, creeping along, like the man was stalking her." He hoped Mrs. Jones would be as impressed with the words as he had been.

Herculeah turned. Her gray eyes burned like embers.

"Well, that is what you said."

"I was being dramatic. Everyone knows I have way too much imagination."

"Did either of you get the license number?"

Herculeah said, "No."

"That's too bad."

"But we got the next best thing," Meat said quickly.

"What's that?"

"His name."

"Meat!" Herculeah said.

"Meat?" Mrs. Jones questioned.

"Roger Cole."

"I'm calling Chico," Herculeah's mother said. She started for the phone.

"I better go home," Meat said. He started for the door, moving slower than Mrs. Jones, giving Herculeah time to call him back. At the door he unzipped his jacket and then zipped it back up, giving Herculeah one more chance.

"Thanks a lot," she said.

The three words struck Meat like stones, but the hard look in her eyes was the bigger blow. He turned and fumbled with the doorknob.

He barely managed to choke out, "You're welcome," before he closed the door behind him.

20

"KCHCHAAH"

"Herculeah!"

Herculeah didn't turn around.

"Herculeah, wait up."

It was after school. Meat and Herculeah usually walked home together. This time she hadn't waited. He finally managed to catch up with her at the corner. But even then, she did not slow down, and he had to run along beside her.

This was the first chance he had gotten to speak to her since that terrible, "Thanks a lot," she had flung at him. He had phoned her three times—no, four, counting the last call when he had hung up without speaking—and three times Mrs. Jones had informed him that Herculeah was studying.

This had left Meat so depressed that he couldn't sleep. He lay in bed imagining the long, lonely years stretching ahead of him in which the girls he was foolish enough to telephone were always studying or painting their nails or washing their hair, doing anything—no matter how tedious—to keep from speaking to him.

He was out of breath from running to catch up with Herculeah, but he gasped out, "I can't come over this afternoon. I've got a dentist appointment."

"Have fun," Herculeah said.

"Herculeah!"

She turned and gave him a cool glance.

She didn't deserve his concern. That was obvious, but he had to give it. "Herculeah," he said, "you really should not go to Elm Street."

"What gives you the idea I'm going there?"

"I know you."

"Not as well as you think you do."

Meat didn't answer.

"Listen, I promised I was not going to put one foot on Elm Street, and I'm not."

"What are you going to do, then?" Meat said. "Stay on the sidewalk?"

At that, Herculeah sighed with apparent disgust

and, working those long legs of hers, disappeared into the crowd.

Meat, now truly depressed, dragged his feet toward Dr. Steinberg's office. He was dreading the sight of the large, white tooth in front of the office on which was written two unreassuring words: TOOTH DOCTOR.

Herculeah dropped her books on the hall table and flopped down on the sofa. She opened her notebook and took out the articles about Amanda Cole's death and the inquest. She reread them although she knew both by heart now.

She focused on the verdict of the jury, that Amanda Cole had met her death from a head injury caused by striking a rock as she fell from her horse.

"I'd like to walk around those old horse trails. I wonder if they're still there," she said to herself. "I'd like to see if I could find where she fell."

Herculeah let the articles drop onto her lap. Her eyes strayed to her granny glasses on the end table. Idly she lifted them and hooked the slim silver loops behind her ears.

Even if I fogged out and got something, I couldn't use it. I can't go back to Elm Street, she said to herself in a childish singsong; then broke off.

She straightened.

Meat was right.

Her feelings toward him softened as she remembered his words, "What are you going to do? Stay on the sidewalk?"

I did promise not to put one foot on Elm Street, Herculeah's thoughts continued. I didn't promise not to check out the horse trails behind Elm Street.

Herculeah took off her glasses. She headed for the front door.

"Thanks, Meat," she said as she glanced at his house. Then she ran down the steps. At the corner she turned in the direction of Elm.

"Kchchaah," Meat said.

Dr. Steinberg said, "I'm almost through, Albert, just a little—"

"Kchchaah," Meat said again, this time accompanying his word with equally unclear gestures.

With a sigh, Dr. Steinberg stopped drilling and said, "What is the trouble, Albert?"

"Dr. Steinberg, I've got to get out of here. A friend of mine's in danger."

"Don't try pulling that again," Dr. Steinberg said wearily.

"This time it's true."

"Open wide, Albert."

"But Dr. Steinberg, she must be in danger. I felt my own hair begin to frizzle."

"You can use hair conditioner like the rest of us. Open wide."

"You don't seem to understand. When Herculeah's hair frizzles, she's in danger. It's like radar hair, Dr. Steinberg. I've got to help her."

"Open wide."

Meat had been in misery ever since he'd been strapped into the dentist's chair—well, he wasn't strapped in, but he might as well have been. He wasn't allowed to get up.

At first it had been because Herculeah was mad at him. That was enough to make anyone miserable.

But then he remembered the way she had looked at him when he had said, "What are you going to do? Stay on the sidewalk?"

That's what she would do—exactly what she would do. At this very moment, she was probably making her way to Elm Street. And here he was, a prisoner in Dr. Steinberg's office. And he had given her the idea. He would be responsible if something happened to her.

Suddenly Meat remembered a conversation he and Herculeah had had last month. It was a phone conversation. They were talking about what one of her next cases might be.

She'd said she'd had a premonition but she didn't want to tell him because it didn't make sense. He'd made her tell him.

"Well," she'd said, "when my mom and I were making a bed for Trip, my mom said to the dog, 'Don't give me that dog-in-the-manger look.'"

"So your premonition has something to do with a dog," he'd said.

"No, the manger! That's what doesn't make any sense. I don't even think there are mangers anymore."

And he had said, "It does make sense. One of Hercules' labors was cleaning a stable. And, Herculeah, that's what a manger is—a stable!"

And now here she was on her way to Elm Street and there were horse trails back in those woods.

Where there were horse trails, there would be stables.

His heart raced with the determination to save Herculeah.

"Kchchaah," he begged frantically.

"I'm almost through, Albert," Dr. Steinberg said.

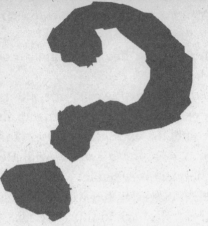

Herculeah came through the woods slowly.

She paused frequently to listen and to glance behind her. She hadn't seen anyone since she had turned into the trees—being very careful not to put one foot on Elm Street—but she had the feeling she needed to be cautious.

From beyond the woods came the sound of bulldozers and tractors, hammers and saws—the comforting sounds of people at work. She couldn't see the construction, but she could hear it, and she was glad it was going on. It helped ease her feeling of isolation.

Herculeah stopped as she came to a wide path that

cut through the woods. It was overgrown with weeds now—no one had walked here in years, much less ridden a horse—yet Herculeah knew this was one of the horse trails. Maybe even the one Amanda Cole had taken that fateful day.

She began to walk the trail, her eyes on the ground. She had no idea what she was looking for—she had been drawn here, the way she had been drawn to the coat in Hidden Treasures. She put her hands in her coat pockets, remembering the note Amanda Cole had written asking for help. Herculeah had no choice but to give it.

She came to a stream and paused. There were rocks here, lots of them. Was it here Amanda Cole's body had been found? She didn't think so. It didn't feel like the place. She kept walking.

And as she walked, her eyes looked from one side of the trail to the other. She continued to ask the question: Here? Did it happen here? She felt she would know it when she came to it.

Herculeah was so intent on her search that gradually she became oblivious to her surroundings.

I really feel that I'm getting close. It's—

A twig snapped, sharp as a rifle shot.

Herculeah stopped, frozen, waiting.

She didn't have to wait long. There was an immediate explosion of noise as something burst through the woods. Herculeah gasped with fright. She whirled around and looked into the face of a Doberman.

The dog was huge. His lips were pulled back into a snarl. Saliva drooled from his mouth. A low growl came from his huge chest.

Herculeah did not move. She did not even breathe.

The growl erupted into fierce barking. The dog came closer. His legs, his whole body was set, tense, eager for the signal to attack. Herculeah could feel the heat of his breath.

"Brute!"

It was a man's voice, and it was a command.

"Back, Brute, back." The man came through the trees, moving quickly. "Back!"

Brute's barks faded into that low, ominous growl. But he didn't move away.

"Down!"

Brute lowered himself to the ground. His lips remained drawn back in a snarl. The low growl continued. Even from his position on the ground, he was ready to spring.

She looked away from the dog and into the eyes of the watchman. This was the man who had tried to run her down. The man who had tried to kill her.

Herculeah said, "I thought your dog was going to attack."

"That's what he's trained to do."

"He frightened me."

"He could have killed you."

The watchman was dressed in work clothes. He was unshaven, unsmiling, and Herculeah knew instinctively that he was even more dangerous than the dog.

"Are you one of the workmen?" she asked through dry lips, though she knew he was not.

He shook his head.

"Oh."

She waited and finally he said, "I'm a watchman. Brute and I make sure there aren't any trespassers. Didn't you see the signs?"

Herculeah said truthfully, "I thought that meant just up where the construction was."

"You were wrong."

"I'm sorry. I—"

"Come with me."

"Look, I'm sorry. I really am. But I need to go home. My mom will be wondering where I am. If you'll just call your dog off—"

"Let's go."

When Herculeah didn't start forward, he said, "Brute." He nodded his head in her direction. "Bring!"

Brute got to his feet at once. He circled Herculeah and came up behind her. Herculeah could feel his hot, wet breath on her hand. The low growling grew louder.

"You'd do well to come on your own," the man said in a deep voice. "He's an attack dog, and he don't like trespassers any more than I do."

Herculeah started forward.

The dog was close behind her. The man led the way. He was so sure of his dog that he didn't bother to glance back.

Herculeah tried to swallow her fear.

Someone will see us, she told herself. Maybe one of the workmen. Someone will come. Meat, maybe, or my mom. Better still, my dad.

Someone will come. Someone has to come.

But until they did, Herculeah knew she had to do exactly what this man told her—if she wanted to live, that is.

And she did. She loved her life.

She loved life as much as—and then came the thought that made her even more afraid—as much as Amanda Cole had.

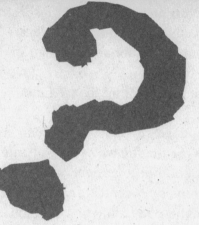

"In there," the man said.

Herculeah balked. Behind her the dog gave an insistent "or-else" bark.

"In there."

Herculeah moved into the room.

She knew where they were—at the long, low building she had seen from the window of the deserted house. This building had once been the stable. The horse stalls were still there at the front, though empty now.

And this room had perhaps held bridles, saddles. It had been the tack room. There was an old iron cot in the corner, but no one had slept on it in years. There were papers on the floor, leaves, trash, straw.

She glanced around quickly to locate an exit, but there was only one door and the man stood in front of it, blocking the way.

Herculeah spun around to face him.

"Sit."

"I'm not a dog," she said with sudden defiance. "You can't command me the way you do Brute."

He did not bother to answer, just stared at her with cold, emotionless eyes. Those were the eyes, Herculeah thought, of a man who could kill.

She glanced around at the cot, but she did not move toward it.

"How long are you going to keep me here?"

"Until I get word."

"From whom?"

"Just word."

"From Roger Cole."

No answer.

"How long will this take? My mom knows where I am. She'll come looking for me."

"It shouldn't be long." He closed the door on her. "I'm leaving Brute outside in case you get any ideas about leaving. Stay," Herculeah heard him tell the dog. "Stay."

Herculeah then heard the sounds of a key being turned and his footsteps walking away.

She found herself in complete darkness. She remembered a line from Amanda Cole's note—"There's no window. I don't know day from night."

Herculeah knew she shared something else with Amanda Cole—a prison.

"Well, at least I'm not drugged," she said aloud. "If I can find a loose board . . ."

She began moving around the room, starting at the baseboard and working her way up to the ceiling, testing each board.

She found one board that was warped. It was waist high. She pulled at it with all her strength. It didn't move.

If only I had some kind of tool . . .

She remembered the iron cot and groped her way toward it. She ran her fingers over it, getting a feel for how it was put together.

The cot was old, rickety. She thought she might be able to—

She put her strength into it. In three strong jerks she had the springs separated from the headboard. And sticking out from the headboard—she felt this with her hands—was the metal bar that held the springs in place. A lever, exactly what she needed.

Again, Herculeah felt her way across the room to the warped board and began to work the metal bar under it. She pried and had the satisfaction of hearing the board pull away from the wall.

She could grip the board now. She wrenched it loose. It would make a weapon—and so would the headboard.

If the man comes back before I get free, I can stand behind the door, and when he comes through—

She took a practice swing.

Of course, she went on, feeling better by the moment, Brute would still be out there, but he might stay by the door. If he was as well trained as he appeared to be, he'd obey his master's command.

I'll worry about the dog when I see daylight, she told herself.

She began work on the next board. It came away even easier than the first.

Other parts of Amanda Cole's note began to throb in her mind.

I don't want to die. I can't die.

The whole building was half-rotten. She would be out of here in no time. She had to be.

He's going to kill me. I know it.

She doubled her efforts.

She was so intent on demolishing the wall and getting out that she did not hear the footsteps outside the door, did not hear the lock being turned, did not hear the command to the dog.

Not until the light from the door lit up the board she struggled with did she remember the last words of the note.

He's back!

23

THE GIRL WHO KNEW TOO MUCH

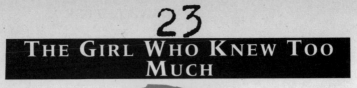

"Hard at work, I see."

The man stepped aside, and Herculeah was face to face with Roger Cole.

Herculeah wanted to throw the iron headboard at him—she was mad enough to—but she restrained herself. She knew it would be useless. She rested her weight against the headboard, keeping it close in case she got a chance to use it later.

"I'm going to get out of here one way or another," she told him.

"Oh, I agree with that."

He smiled. His smile wasn't dazzling now. It was

threatening. Yet there was a look in his eyes that let Herculeah know he was enjoying what he was doing.

"I hoped I'd seen the last of you," he said. "I hoped that my apology would end it."

"It didn't."

"So I see."

The man with the dog stood behind him, watching. If Herculeah got past Roger Cole, she'd have him and Brute to contend with.

"Well." Herculeah shrugged and managed a smile. "I guess I was being silly—playing Nancy Drew. If you'll call the dog off, I'll go on home."

Roger Cole watched her. His look sharpened as he took in her expression. "You weren't just playing Nancy Drew, were you?"

She did not answer.

"It had something to do with the coat, didn't it?" He watched her thoughtfully.

Herculeah didn't answer.

"How did you get the coat, anyway?"

She could tell him that much. And she needed time.

"I bought it."

"Where?"

"From a store called Hidden Treasures. The owner of the shop said it came in a box of horse gear."

Roger Cole smashed one hand against the side of the door. He didn't turn to look at the man behind him as he spoke. "You stupid . . . Why didn't you check what went out of here?"

"I did."

"Obviously not good enough."

He looked at Herculeah. "You bought the coat."

"Yes."

"And?"

"There was a note from your aunt in the lining of the coat—she'd pushed it through a hole in the pocket. The note told everything. I showed the note to my father. He's a police detective," Herculeah said with more confidence than she felt. "So it won't do any good to get rid of me."

"Maybe you did show it to him. Maybe you didn't."

"This is where you held her prisoner, isn't it?" Herculeah went on, buying time.

Roger Cole did not answer.

"This had to be the room. In the note she said there was no window, and she couldn't tell night from day. When you closed the door on me, I couldn't either.

"I think I know how it happened," Herculeah went on in a normal tone of voice, though inwardly she yelled for Meat, her mother, her father, a workman, somebody, anybody to come.

"Your aunt slept there." She glanced toward the dismantled cot. "You drugged her, kept her prisoner here until she signed. . . . What did she sign?"

"You know everything," Roger Cole said. He was not smiling now. "You tell me."

Herculeah's look was thoughtful as she remembered the note. "You kept her prisoner until she signed some papers." A light came into her gray eyes. "Until she signed the papers allowing you to have the land. That's it, isn't it? You wanted to develop the property and she didn't."

"The girl knows too much," the man murmured to Roger Cole. Roger Cole seemed to agree.

"You wanted to chop up her land and put houses on it. She wouldn't have that, would she? She loved this place, loved the flowers, the trees, loved to ride the trails."

"How do you know so much about her?"

"We're a lot alike."

"Same size, anyway. You're more of a fighter."

"She might have been, too, if she hadn't been drugged." She gave him a scornful look. "And all the while you were putting on the big pretense of being the loving nephew. You took her meals up, you did everything for her. And all the while she was alone, a prisoner out here in this terrible room."

"And if you are right? It doesn't really make any difference. You aren't going anywhere. Suppose I did keep her prisoner, you have no proof."

"There may be proof right here." Herculeah looked

around her. "I think you killed her here. She was too weak to get on a horse. You—" Instinctively her eyes shifted from Roger Cole to the watchman. She knew now that it was the watchman who had killed and Roger Cole who had directed it. "You killed her here, saddled the horse, led it down the trail to a likely spot, dumped the body, and let the horse go free."

"She knows too much," the watchman said again.

"I agree, but—"

At that moment Herculeah heard the most wonderful sound she had ever heard in her life: an earsplitting, head-bursting whistle.

Only Meat could whistle like that.

The two men turned their heads in the direction of the whistle. That was Herculeah's moment.

She threw the headboard at Roger Cole with all her strength. It knocked him backward. At the same time she screamed, "Get away from me! Get away!"

She hoped the two men would think she was talking to them.

Actually her warning was to Meat. If he came down here, they'd both end up victims of Brute.

The watchman moved swiftly. He stepped around Roger Cole, and in a second slammed Herculeah against the inside wall of the stable. It knocked the breath out of her. She saw stars.

"Brute!" he yelled.

Brute came.

"Guard!"

Brute was in front of her now, his face so close Herculeah's heart leapt with fear.

"If you move, he'll kill you."

Her mind, shocked into a stupor, barely took in the words.

He repeated them.

"If you move, he'll kill you."

Herculeah blinked her eyes.

"If you call out, he'll kill you."

The man watched for a moment, making sure she had taken in his meaning. Then he shut the door. Herculeah heard the sound of a key in the lock. She was left in darkness with only the terrible sound of Brute's eager breathing.

And as the men walked away, the watchman said, "And if he don't, I will."

24

BRUTE FORCE

Meat heard Herculeah's cry.

"Get away from me! Get away!"

He heard the desperation in her voice, and his heart pounded. He knew that Herculeah was in some sort of terrible danger and that he would be in danger if he went closer.

He stood for a moment where he was, in the shadow of the elm trees. His knees had begun to shake, and he leaned against the tree for support.

Meat had come to Elm Street directly from the dentist's office. First he had borrowed the dentist's phone and called Herculeah's home. He had had a brief, unsatisfactory conversation with Herculeah's mom.

"Is Herculeah there?" he'd asked.

"No, Meat, where is she?"

"I don't know. That's what I called to find out. Did she come home after school?"

"Where is she?"

There was a pause, then she reworded the question. "Meat, where do you think she is?"

"I don't know. At the stables."

"What stables?"

"I wish I knew."

"What stables, Meat?"

Now Herculeah's mother was yelling at him. Even the patients sitting across the room heard her.

"Maybe Elm Street. But I don't know for sure. That's just a maybe."

Mrs. Jones must have found the conversation as frustrating as he did because at that point she slammed down the phone.

The patients heard that, too, and nobody looked at him as he made his way from the office.

Now Meat twisted his hands in indecision. He knew Herculeah had come to danger, as he had feared, in the stable. Why, why hadn't he called Lieutenant

Jones? That's who he should have called—not Mrs. Jones, who served subpoenas and found kidnapped dogs. And if he left to call him now, Herculeah might be gone when he got back.

Meat ran to the street where the workmen were knocking off for the day. Meat always felt inferior around construction workers, even though he was as big as some of them.

He approached a tall man in jeans and a backward Braves cap who was getting into his truck. Only his desperation for Herculeah gave him the courage to say, "Excuse me."

"Yeah?"

"I thought I heard some cries for help back in the woods—down by the stable. It sounded like a girl I know. Would you mind— Would it be too much trouble— Could you possibly—"

"Want me to take a look? Sure. Hey, Sam, let's check this out," he called to a fellow workman. "This kid heard some cries for help."

"Right, Cobby."

Meat felt a lot better about approaching the stable now that he was flanked by Sam and Cobby.

"The cry came from back here," he said, pointing the way to the stable.

As they got closer, Meat's alarm grew. The stable looked deserted.

"That's funny," Meat said. "There were two men standing here."

"Door's padlocked," Sam said.

"Herculeah? Herculeah!"

No answer.

"That's the name of the girl I heard yelling for help."

"With a name like that, she ought to be able to take care of herself."

"Usually she can. Herculeah!"

Again there was no answer.

The workmen walked slowly around the stable. At the back, they called, "Hey, anybody here? Hello!"

Slowly they returned to where Meat was standing by the door.

"Kid, we don't hear a thing."

"But I really did hear a cry for help," Meat said. "I did. I promise."

"Well, it doesn't look like help's needed now."

The men turned to go.

"Wait," Meat said. "There's somebody inside. Put your ear against the door. You can hear breathing."

"I'll check. Anybody in there?" Cobby called. "You need help in there?"

"Maybe she's unconscious and can't answer. Maybe she's tied up or gagged. Maybe—"

Cobby raised one hand to cut him off. He put his head against the door.

"Yeah, I hear something, all right."

"Breathing?" Meat asked.

"It's more like a low rumbling. Growling—something like that. Check it out, Sam."

Sam put his head against the door.

"There's a dog in there. That's a growling dog." He stepped back. "We can't open that door. That's an attack dog. I've seen him with the watchman—big, strong Doberman. Teeth like a crocodile."

"If you'll break the door down, I'll help," Meat offered.

"Kid, you haven't seen this dog."

"I've seen dogs before."

"Not like this."

Again the two workers turned away. Meat followed, keeping up with them, saying, "Please! I think my friend may be locked in with the dog. My friend's in there with that dog. We can't leave her."

"What makes you think your friend's in there?"

"That's where I heard her voice."

Meat wiped his hands on his pants. "Listen, will you do me one favor—just one favor?"

Cobby held up both hands. "I don't want anything to do with that dog."

"Me either," Sam said. "I mean, this is an attack dog, kid. Attack dogs go for the throat. They don't shake your pants leg like the average ticked-off dog."

"I know that."

"I am not taking on any dog," Cobby said forcefully. "That's final."

"You won't have to."

Meat eyed the tools on Sam's belt. "I just want you to take that hammer and smash the lock. Then you can go on, and I'll take the blame. I'd do it myself if I could."

Sam came forward. "Just break the lock, huh?"

"Yes."

"And you won't open the door till me and Cobby are ten miles up the road?"

"Yes."

Sam pulled a hammer from his belt. "I want to get one thing straight, kid. You never saw me and you never saw this hammer."

"That's right."

Sam lifted the hammer and in one incredible, well-aimed blow, sent the lock flying. At the noise the dog was at the door, barking fiercely, frantically. His claws dug at the wood.

Sam said, "It's all yours, kid."

25

BACK AGAINST THE WALL

Herculeah could not move. She could not call for help. Her back was to the wall.

Up until the moment when Sam smashed the lock, the Doberman had been directly in front of her, letting out a low, continuous growl. The room reeked of his breath.

With the crashing of the lock, the dog had left her and gone to attack the door. Still, Herculeah dared not move or speak. Before Roger Cole and the watchman left they had told her that the dog was trained to attack if she did either.

Even now, with the whole length of the room be-tween her and the dog, she dared not cry out.

"Herculeah, I'm out here!" Meat called. He was wip-ing his hands on his pants. "I'm going to help you." He dried his hands again. He felt he could dry them for the rest of his life and not get the sweat off.

He heard footsteps behind him and froze. He couldn't bring himself to turn around. He knew the watchman and Roger Cole were back. Now they would throw him into the room with Herculeah and the dog, and he was just the kind of person dogs loved to attack—sweaty and scared and—

"It's us again," a voice said.

Meat turned and faced Cobby and Sam. He almost crumbled to the ground with relief.

"Yeah, we never did know when to leave well enough alone."

"Thank you," Meat gasped. It was the most inade-quate phrase in the English language. "I mean really thank you." That still wasn't good enough.

"Sam here was mentioning that he noticed some loose boards on the back of the building when he was walking around. He got the idea we could pry one off."

"Yeah, the building's going to be torn down in a week or two anyway."

"We get one board off, we can look in. If we don't see your friend, we nail it back on."

"What if we do see her?" Meat asked.

"We'll worry about it then, okay? Let's get going, kid."

Meat followed the construction workers around to the back of the stable. To Meat, construction workers were the heroes of the world. If he could have chosen any profession for his missing father, it would have been construction. These weren't big men, but they had a certain power in their movements that he admired.

At the back of the stable Sam and Cobby made quick work of the loose boards. But all they could see was the terrible snarling face of Brute that filled the opening.

"Get out of the way, you," Cobby said, punching the dog with the handle of his hammer.

In a movement so quick it took them all by surprise, the Doberman turned his head sideways, snapped at the handle, and pulled the hammer through the hole.

"Hey, that's my hammer," Cobby said.

"Man, that dog'll even attack a hammer."

The dog dropped the hammer, and his face appeared almost instantly in the opening, but in the second it had taken him to drop the hammer, Meat had seen the pale face of Herculeah against the far wall.

"I see you, Herculeah," he cried. "We're going to help you."

Cobby said, "Sam, you keep the dog occupied."

"With what? He's already got my hammer."

"With sticks, anything. What'd you say the girl's name was?"

"Herculeah."

"Hey, Herc," Sam called into the opening.

Meat knew that Herculeah did not allow anyone to call her that, but he thought she might make an exception for construction workers.

"We're going to keep the dog occupied, hon. You slip on around the wall if you can. Just inch around, real slow. Get right by the door. We'll give you a count and then we'll open the door just enough for you to slip through. Don't try to answer me. Just try to do it."

"Get me some sticks, kid—big ones."

Glad for something to do, Meat ran around gathering up the biggest sticks he could find and bringing them to where Sam stood at the back of the stable.

"I hope this works."

Sam shoved one of the sticks into the hole and instantly it was yanked out of his hand. The dog's snarling face appeared in the hole, his teeth bared, saliva and foam dripping from his mouth.

"Man, he is tough on sticks," Sam said, feeding him another.

"Can you see my friend?" Meat asked anxiously.

"I can't see much of anything but dog," Sam said. "Ugly dog."

He fed him another stick.

Sam said to Meat, "This is like a machine my wife ordered that crunches up sticks to make mulch. Man, this dog can make mulch. Look at that."

"You got the dog occupied?" Cobby called from the front of the stable.

"As long as my sticks hold out."

"Can you see my friend?" Meat tried to peer around the dog.

"Yeah, she's making her way toward the door. More sticks! More sticks!"

Herculeah inched slowly toward the door. Her heart pounded. Her legs were like rubber, too weak to support her. She was aware that at any moment the Doberman could turn and attack.

She had heard the construction worker say, "Attack dogs go for the throat."

Back against the rough wall, she inched toward the door. She was at the corner now. She turned.

Still the dog had not looked around. At his feet was a pile of shredded sticks. His antagonism with the man seemed to be growing.

Another inch.

And another.

Herculeah kept her eyes on the dog. Don't turn, she willed him. Don't turn. I'm almost there. Whatever you do, don't turn.

"She's at the door, Cobby," Sam called.

Meat ran around the stable and waited at Cobby's elbow.

Cobby said, "I'm going to count, hon. And when I get to three, I'm going to push the door open and pull you out. Ready?"

Herculeah wasn't sure. Her knees were weak. Her throat was dry. Her heart pounded in her ears.

"One!"

Herculeah tried to ready herself. She knew she would have to make the move of her life.

"Two!"

Herculeah took a deep breath. Power flowed into her weak legs, her trembling arms. She had never been readier for anything in her life.

"Three!"

26

THE THREE OF THEM

The door opened.

Strong fingers encircled Herculeah's arm, and in a move that was so fast Meat couldn't see it even though he was standing right there, Herculeah came hurtling out the door.

Cobby pulled the door shut behind her just as the dog hurled himself against it.

"If this door had opened out instead of in, that dog would be on top of us, strong as he is." He looked down at Herculeah. "You all right, hon? I didn't mean to pull you so hard."

"It was just right. They were going to kill me," Herculeah said. "They were really going to kill me."

She trembled, and Cobby patted her. "You're safe. Don't collapse on me now."

"I won't."

"We're not out of here yet."

Sam came around the stable. "That is one mad dog. He's trying to chew the stable down. He's gnawing at those boards. I don't want to be around here when he breaks out."

"Let's get out of here," Cobby said.

"Fine with me," Meat said quickly.

"Can you make it to my truck, hon?"

Herculeah nodded.

Now that Herculeah was up and out of danger, Meat felt useless. Sure, he had been the one to get the construction workers, but they were the heroes.

Ahead of him, it was Herculeah who had a construction worker on either side of her. He watched her give a shaky laugh as if to belittle her fears.

Meat could appreciate the terror of being locked in a room with an attack Doberman. Meat had never had a dog and didn't particularly care for them. He wondered sometimes about people who actually chose to have an animal living in their house.

Meat had gotten a whiff of the air that Herculeah

had breathed for the hour she awaited rescue, and that had been enough to turn him off dogs for life. The phrase "dog breath" had a whole new meaning for Meat.

Ahead of him Herculeah cried, "Oh, there's my mom, my mom! And my dad!"

Herculeah struggled up the hill toward them. Meat continued his lonely progress up the hill. He hoped he would be able to get a ride home with the Joneses. Herculeah was getting all the sympathy—which she certainly deserved—but his legs were weak, too.

Herculeah's mother was out of the car now, running toward her. "Are you all right?" She hugged Herculeah and then pulled back to look at her.

"Oh, Mom."

"Don't 'Oh, Mom' me. I've been frantic. Where were you? Where was she?" She decided she had a better chance of getting the truth from the construction workers.

"I don't want to worry you, ma'am, but she was locked up with a Doberman. I wouldn't wish that on my worst enemy."

"A Doberman? A dog?"

"Attack dog."

"Oh, Mom, Dad, I have so much to tell you." She broke away from her mother's embrace to hug her dad. "Dad, Roger Cole did it."

"What?"

"Killed Amanda Cole. And when he knew I knew, he locked me in with the Doberman. They were coming back later to kill me, if the Doberman didn't do it for them. These guys saved my life."

"Slow down," her father said.

"Well, remember I found that letter in the lining of Amanda Cole's coat?"

"Well," Cobby interrupted, realizing it was going to be a long story, "hon, if you're taken care of, me and Sam will be on our way." He turned to Herculeah's father. "If you need us, we'll be here tomorrow, on the job—just ask for Sam and Cobby."

"From what little Herculeah's said, I understand you helped her, and I'd like to thank you."

"Our pleasure. She's quite a gal."

"I'll check with you tomorrow."

Meat joined the scene just as Herculeah turned to Sam and Cobby. And then she said something Meat would remember for the rest of his life.

"You men were just wonderful." Her gray eyes, shining now with tears, turned to include him. "All three of you."

27
DOUBLE DUTY

"Meat," Herculeah said, "do you think that some-where in the world there is someone exactly like you?"

"Oh, I hope not," Meat said without thinking, "for their sake." Then he added quickly, "I mean, one of me is enough."

Herculeah was talking on the phone to Meat. "Now don't talk long. Your father's going to call," her mother had said.

"I'll hang up as soon as I hear a beep."

Herculeah continued. "Well, Meat, the reason I was asking is because I felt such a kinship with Amanda Cole. It wasn't just that she was my size. It was—oh, I can't explain it. If you haven't had the feeling—and you obviously haven't—well . . ."

"Do you think your dad's going to nail Roger Cole and the watchman?" Meat said, abruptly changing the subject, because he wasn't enjoying the one they had.

"Yes."

"But I remember that your father said it was sort of a policeman's belief that if he didn't nail his killer inside of a week, his chances of ever getting him were divided by half for every week that passed—something mathematical like that—and this has been years!"

"My dad also believes that no murderer ever left the scene of the crime without leaving some physical evidence behind him. If it's there, my dad'll find it. Didn't you see the expression on his face?"

"He didn't have any expression."

"That's the whole point. Meat, that's when my dad's really dangerous. His face gets like a mask. It's almost scary. It got like that when he found out I'd been shut up with the Doberman, and I knew then that he'd nail those two men somehow.

"If nothing else, he can get them on what they did to me—aggravated assault and intent to commit bodily harm. But that's not good enough. I want him to get them for murdering Amanda Cole. I promised."

"You couldn't really promise. She's dead."

"A promise to a dead person is more binding than any other. Oh, and I have to tell you about my mom. She made me start from the beginning. I told about finding the note and the key, and she exploded. 'Not another key! Haven't you learned your lesson about keys? You find a key, you find a body. First it was Dead Oaks. Then Madame Rosa . . .' There's no reasoning with her when she gets like this. I said, 'Mom, the key is useless. The lock is gone.' But I had to go upstairs, get the key, come back, and—"

There was a beep and Herculeah said quickly, "Oh, someone's trying to call. It's probably my dad. I'll call you back."

Meat hung up the phone. He continued to sit there. He looked at his watch. Time moved so slowly when he was waiting for a call from Herculeah, and then when the call came, it would be over in a minute.

The house was too quiet. Even when nothing was happening at Herculeah's, her house didn't feel this quiet.

He looked at his watch again. He would have thought it had stopped if the second hand hadn't been moving.

When the phone rang, finally, Meat picked it up on the first ring.

Herculeah said, "My dad got them. I knew he would. He got them!"

"He's arrested them?"

"Yes!"

"Both of them?"

"Yes, and guess what the evidence is?"

"I can't."

"Remember the last two words of Amanda Cole's note?"

"No."

"'Look inside.' Remember, I kept wondering what that could mean? Then, when I went in the house, that's what was so distressing—there was nothing left that anything could be inside of."

"Yes."

"Well, there was something left. And there were more sheets from the address book inside. Guess where?"

"Give me a clue."

"They were inside the mattress of that old cot in the stable. When I tore the bed apart, trying to get a weapon or tool of some kind, the mattress fell on the floor and the pages all came tumbling out.

"I didn't see them because it was dark, but my dad did. He says it's all there—all the proof he needs."

Meat was still going over it in his mind when Herculeah said, "Well, I've got to go."

"Already? We just got started."

"My father is coming over to give me one of his lectures."

Meat wished his father would come over, even for a lecture.

"But let me just say one more thing," Meat added, not wanting the conversation to end.

"Sure."

"When I was at the dentist's office, I had a premonition about stables. Remember, one of Hercules' labors was cleaning the Augean stables."

"I know."

"But now I'm wondering if, instead, it could be the watchdog! Another of Hercules' labors was bringing Cerberus, the watchdog, from hell."

"That does describe the Doberman."

"I agree."

"Hey, maybe I did two labors in one—double duty," Herculeah said, grinning to herself. "Even Hercules didn't do two at the same time."

"Maybe. Anyway, you've still got a long way to go." He paused. "And you don't have any premonitions?"

"About the next one?"

"Yes."

"If I tell you, you'll tease me."

"No, no, I won't. I never tease people because I know how bad it feels to be teased. Have I ever teased you?"

"No."

"So tell me."

"Oh, all right. A bull." There was silence, then Herculeah went on quickly. "I know what you're thinking. You're thinking that I'm still hung up on stables, that I couldn't possibly be threatened by a bull, that I'm—"

"No, that is not what I'm thinking," Meat said, interrupting. "I'm thinking the Cretan bull."

"What?"

"Capturing the Cretan bull—that was one of Hercules' labors."

"Well, I don't know what a Cretan bull is, and I can't explain why I know this, but, well, this is a different kind of bull. But just as—"

She broke off.

"Just as what?"

"Deadly," Herculeah said.

There was another pause while Herculeah's hair started to rise and Meat's fears did, too. Herculeah forced herself to laugh. "Anyway, can a bull be any more dangerous than a Doberman?"

"We'll probably find out."

"Good night, Meat."

"Good night, Herculeah."